BLOOD BEACH

by

Adam Hardy

THUNDERCHILD PUBLISHING
Huntsville, Alabama

This is a work of fiction. All of the characters, organizations, and events portrayed in this novel are either products of the author's imagination or are used fictitiously.

BLOOD BEACH

ISBN-13: 978-1530458318
ISBN-10: 1530458315

Published by Thunderchild Publishing
1898 Shellbrook Drive
Huntsville, AL 35806

Cover design by Dan Thompson

Table of Contents

Dedication

For
BRIAN CORMACK

Chapter One

Trust Fox to get himself blown up on his birthday.

High through the air flew George Abercrombie Fox, end over end. His eyelids snapped up. Flame and fire, fire and flame, sheets and gouts and roaring infernos of fire burst upwards from the three burning ships. Fox saw the blazing vessels cartwheeling about him as he span through the air.

The water revolving below him beckoned with inky darkness in the troughs and burnished orange flakes of reflected fire flamed from the crests. The noise had passed comprehension. The air burned in his lungs.

Down he plunged, plummeting towards the sea.

In the moments before he struck the water Fox felt the quick stab of pain from his buttocks and so knew he'd really done it, done what he'd so sourly promised he never would do.

He'd caught his trousers alight, there on the quarterdeck of his late command, the fireship *Nuthatch.*

The water smashed cold at him. He fought his way to the surface and broke through into the churning waters of the bay, now a cauldron of lurid light. He shook his head, feeling the cold biting at him. He'd been blown up in the instant he'd dived for safety; apart from the sting in his tail, he appeared to be unharmed.

Back there in the inlet, *Nuthatch,* with her artfully arranged freight of combustibles and powder, burned and roared, and in her voluntary destruction enwrapped in mutual destruction the two French frigates that had been the prime cause of all this deadly activity. Now the mad Corsican bandit Bonaparte possessed two less vessels, was short of two powerful and dangerous vessels to aid him in his struggle against England. What damage those two heavy frigates might have done across the tenuous sea links of England's merchant marine did not bear contemplation; happily, now that Fox had burned them, contemplation of that unfruitful kind was no longer necessary.

Commander Fox would have taken great comfort from that in other circumstances; now he had to make shift to get himself out of his predicament. He could swim all the way back across the bay to the English vessels if needs be; but the French guard boats would be pulling around, looking for men in the water. Fox had not the least desire to spend the rest of this war, wretched though it might be, stowed away and forgotten in some stinking Frog prison.

The breath had come back to his lungs now and he could breathe again. He felt as though he'd fallen onto the hatch from the main crosstrees of a three-decker; but he'd live. He struck out away from the inlet where the three burning ships drifted, spouting gobbets of fire into the night sky, trailing a plume of smoke that would choke into the lungs and sting the eyes of the people of Point Avenglas. With a lean, economical stroke he swam for the open sea.

The massive shape of the block-ship passed away on his right. The two British fireships had not burned the hulk, so Fox

6

had been forced to take his blazing *Nuthatch* through the gap and on into the inlet to burn the two frigates.

Somewhere out across the bay his crew must be pulling for the sea and the English vessels.

The scene about him would have fired up the heart of Dante.

The fires, the massive concussions of guns, the shrieking of men, the plunging hiss of red-hot shot, all blended into a mad diapason of warlike passion and military insanity. Scenes of this nature had been part and parcel of Fox's life ever since he'd been read into the books of the old *Henrietta* as a powder monkey.

Well, he'd damned well done his duty, and he was, for the moment, still alive. And, too, bigod — it was his birthday!

Above the bedlam he heard the crack of a musket, so near was the shot. The ball spat spitefully into the water close by his head. Fox took a breath, dived, and kicked his way underwater, holding his breath with that fearsome ease that made guffawing sailormen dub him a merman. He surfaced some way further on and settled down to his swimming rhythm again.

As old Swede had said, shaking his blond head: "It's a mortal cruel thing for a sailor to know how to swim, young Abe. It only prolongs the agony."

He was well past the block-ship now and striking into the centre of the bay. Lost in the darkness above the fire-spattered waters rose the cliffs surrounding the bay of Point Avenglas. Up there he and Etienne, the spy, had taken observations of this anchorage and so marked for capture or destruction the two frigates that now burned in fulfilment of the plan.

Chips of reflected fire flaked from the crests of the waves as he swam. The plan had been fulfilled, yes; but only in its second best form. Old Admiral Cloughton, coughing and wheezing, had wanted those two French frigates cut out. He'd wanted them sailed back out of the bay and into the welcoming embrace of the Royal Navy. That would have been a fine affair indeed and, apart from the honour and glory, which were cheap enough, God knew, in this confounded war, there would have been prize money to share out. As it was the boats had muffed their chances at the boom and so Fox had been forced to go it alone, following phase-two of the plan, and burn the frigates.

Never a man to relish the destruction of a fine ship, Fox could feel sorrow for beautiful vessels burned intermingled with his furious wrath that he'd once more been cheated of some useful prize money.

The coldness of the water, this late in September, struck at him shrewdly. He saw the vague outlines of the boat ahead with mingled relief and caution. There were boats strewn all over the bay, wreckage adrift, dead men afloat, all the grisly aftermath of the carnage caused by the failure of the British boats to break through.

Fox drew up to the boat with great caution.

He paddled around it carefully. He could see no sign of occupancy, no heads and shoulders above the gunwale, no arms pulling oars. He took a breath, put his square powerful hands on the transom and with an eel-like squirm hauled himself up. He chested the transom and looked into the shadows within the boat.

If some skulking French soldier or sailor was preparing to bring a cutlass or a pistol barrel down on his head — why, Fox was used to that. He was ready. Nothing happened. The boat rocked listlessly.

Some distance across the bay to starboard the burning hulk of His Britannic Majesty's gunbrig *Glowworm* cast spouts of fire heavenwards. The fire was a pale glimmer in comparison to the gigantic cauldron aft where *Nuthatch* and the frigates burned. In the glow Fox saw shadows writhing in the bottom of the boat. He saw the orange-runnelled gleam from steel.

He got a knee over the transom, heaved and so slid on to the stern-sheets. The boat was capacious, large, and he knew already it was French. Up in the bows a two-pounder snouted uglily. He moved forward, warily, looking down.

There were three soldiers and two sailors on the bottom boards or tangled over the thwarts; and they were all dead.

A part of the gunwale had been chewed as though by a berserk terrier dog. Grape had done that. This boat had been rowing guard duty, and had tangled with one of the British boats. The exchange of fire in the darkness had slain most of the crew and the soldiers, and those who had not been killed outright had been taken off by another French boat — or so reckoned G. A. Fox.

Fox filled his lungs. The water-drenched shirt and trousers clung to him. He did not shiver; but he knew damn well he'd relish the end of the night's work and a shift into clothes which, although damp as always aboard ship, would be drier than these. He heaved up the bodies and rifled their pockets, for in matters of this kind Fox thought first of his responsibilities to his family of Foxes by the Thames — that crew of aged aunts, and sisters, and brothers, and babies and sisters-and brothers-in-law, and of his mother — and even the few coins he found would help. Then, and with a short word over each, he bundled the corpses over the side.

Now he had himself a boat, a command, again.

The French, caught up in the madness of the fighting, would have taken their men off to man the fighting boats. They could always pick up this relic in the morning, for then the British would be gone. There were three oars. Philosophically, Fox stuck the soundest looking of the three over the stern and began to scull. As he worked the blade from side to side in the water, giving it that cunning feathering twist, and the boat took

9

up way and moved ahead, he reflected that cold though he was, this was a far more satisfactory method of reaching the English ships than swimming.

The boat's progress was slow, for she was a largish lump for one man to propel. He worked away and felt his clothes drying on him. He could do this all night, if needs be, even after all the excitements and exertions of bringing his fire-ship into Point Avenglas. That was what being a naval officer was all about.

If he bumped into a French guard boat, of course, the whole picture would change dramatically.

Although the staff in the stern had been shot away and no colours flew there any longer, Fox had cunning and somewhat vicious ideas on what he would do if challenged by a Frenchman.

Using economical and powerful strokes, Fox propelled the boat towards safety. His short chunky body balanced perfectly and his massive muscles rolled with just the right amount of exertion. His breathing remained steady and rhythmical.

No more flares rose from the land, but Fox did not for a moment suppose the French had run out of rockets. They knew well enough by now that the main item on the night's agenda had been passed. The infernal English had attacked, and been beaten off, and a maniac in a blazing fireship had sailed in and burned the precious frigates. Now it would be a matter of courts martial and punishments and God alone knew what for the Frogs. Fox bore them no ill will. As he sculled along he knew well enough he'd kill any Frenchman who tried to take this boat from him, just as he knew that in other circumstances he'd be only too happy to sit drinking cognac with a Frenchman and sing raucous, bawdy songs all night with him.

Glowworm still burned, although the gun-vessel's flickering light cast ever decreasing illumination across the black waters. There were boats still pulling across the bay, and occasionally amidst the slackening gunfire Fox heard a yell and a shrill reply. He had to be careful. The forts had given up shooting at the English frigates and gun-vessels. The block-ship fell silent. Now the roaring hiss as the ships in the inlet burned reached him with a crackling roar, very shivery.

The set of the ebb was helping him now; and in pushing him along, it gave him a chance to ease up the savagery of his attack on the oar. He could take smoother strokes now, steering, using the moon-drawn waters to full advantage.

By this time the boat from *Nuthatch* should have got well clear, taking Grey and Carker and the crew to safety. Those two lieutenants of his, John Carker and Lionel Grey, had solemnly doffed their hats and wished him a happy birthday, there on the quarterdeck as the fireship bore in to the attack, smashed and battered by red-hot shot. Bigod! They were a pair. And his crew, all of them, for there had remained only the one boat to take them off, would have gone down all the way amid the fire had he not summarily ordered them off.

There was little wonder that as George Abercrombie Fox, Commander in the Royal Navy, thirty-five years of age as he was on this very day, sculled himself away from the holocaust, his mind should begin to mull over what prospects of future employment lay ahead.

All the time he pondered what that future might bring — flashes of thought all mixed up with Admiral Cloughton and Percy Staunton, with Lord Kintlesham and his daughter, Sophy, with his family and his crew — he also kept both his eyes skinned. Both eyes were working very well. He could see the flickering glimmer across the water, lights beginning to show ashore as the French breathed again, the damned English having gone, and he was aware of the longer finger of illumination stretching and dancing across the water from the burning ships. The darkness closed in.

Fox strained his eyes ahead.

Dim shadows moving — clumps of darkness within darkness — a heaving movement of shadowy forms — the subtle suggestion of mass and body out there across the water ... He stared and dashed a hand across his face, and so stared out again, his nose arrogantly beaked, his chin set, all his powerful body eloquent of the savage barbarian accosted by foes.

Instinctively, with all the cunning of his nature, Fox angled his boat out and away from that ominous clumping of shadows ahead. He just wanted to get well away. He had no wish to become embroiled in more fighting. The idea of a good stiff tot of rum struck him as a capital notion, along with that almost dry shirt and trousers and the cot he'd find somewhere in Captain Sandeman's *Alarm.*

Standing up like this in a white shirt made him an easy figure to see, particularly in the darkness shot through with random gleams from the fires. He wanted to crouch down and conceal himself; but he continued to stand up, steadily sculling and steering. And, furthermore, Fox now put a great deal more effort into each stroke of the oar.

He heard excited French voices, all swearing away in the new argot that had become fashionable after the Terror and since the nominal notion of almighty God had been swept away from the poor benighted Frog minds. From deluded Papists they'd become deluded atheists; Fox listened. His retentive mind picked up the expressions and the oaths, stored them all away. You never knew when just this kind of information might not become invaluable.

Listening intently, sculling with purpose, Fox kept his eyes fixed on that amorphous mass ahead. His change of course brought the shadow on to his starboard bow. *Glowworm* still burned. As he sculled onwards the French boat passed between

12

Fox and the burning gun-vessel. The shape did not look like any reasonable boat Fox would recognise. He peered closer.

There were two boats over there.

In the same instant as he realised that highly significant fact, an outburst of shouting and a popping fusillade of pistol and musket shots spattered up into the night sky.

Among all the yelling and banging, Fox heard, quite clearly, a stentorian voice yell: "Bash him on the head, Barnabas! Mr. Grey — your back!"

Fox sighed.

So his crew hadn't gone pulling blindly for the sea. They hadn't obeyed their orders. Mr. Carker and Mr. Grey should have taken the boat out to sea to rejoin the little English squadron. Had they done so they would not now be here, in the centre of the bay, fiercely battling a French guard boat chock-full of men.

Again Fox sighed.

The roaring devils had waited for him, most likely had been pulling up against the ebb to fish him out of the water.

That being so — why were they so late?

Fox looked again, more sharply, straining his eyes to pick out details against the dying glare of *Glowworm.*

The French boat bulked huge and aggressive among the shadows; the English boat lay low in the water.

So that was the answer!

An abrupt spurt of fire and a following concussion from the inlet aft told him that one of the French frigates had at last blown up.

Fox did not look back.

He kept his eyes fixed on those two boats and as the illumination belched in orange fury across the water he saw all the details he needed and instantly had seen what he must do.

Anyway, to a man who had seen *l'Orient* blow up in Abukir Bay no ship explosion would ever be the same again.

The two boats were not yet grappled over there. The pistol shots rang out, short sharp spiteful cracks in the night. The English were holding the French off in defiance of their superior numbers, and from a sinking boat beneath them. Fox scrambled forward and in the flickering erratic glow from the abruptly magnified conflagration saw what he needed all neatly laid out in the bows. Trust the French to do a workmanlike job when it came to organising a guard boat.

The flint and steel were to hand. The little two-pounder was already loaded as the marker told him at his impatient thrust down the barrel. He seized a canvas bag of langrage and stuffed that down on top. His face, as ugly and devilish as ever, bore a look of unholy evil. Let the Frogs bite on that little lot!

The difficulty lay in manoeuvring the boat with the single oar over the stern and then in lunging forrard and firing the gun whilst the bows still pointed at the target. But if Fox could do nothing else in life, he could handle a boat.

Carrying all three boats with it, the ebb swept on. Fox sculled so that the sweat started out all over his body. He scarcely noticed it. He had to get this damned sea-scow so positioned that he could use the bow gun. He knew what was happening over there, where the two boats grew in size and clarity of outline against the orange glimmer off the water,

The British boat, waterlogged, sinking, probably only barely kept afloat by constant hectic baling, was being tormented and shot at by the French, who kept their distance after their first attempt at carrying the boat by a rush. All the English pistols would be wet through and useless. His men were being forced to sit still under a galling fire. Fox felt the fire in him, felt the anger forcing his muscles to crack as he thrust savagely at the oar. Bigod! No fancy Monsieur Jean Crapaud was going to murder his crew and get away with it! He'd see Johnny Crapaud dead and ten fathoms under and the fishes eating his eyes out first!

Now he had the two shapes disentangled, a strip of water between the hulls. In the confusing darkness with fire streaks from burning vessels his only illumination, it was difficult to see straight. But there was a dreadful discrepancy in the free-board of the two boats. The French boat rode normally; the British boat was almost gunwales under.

If Grey and Carker hadn't got the men in the water inside the boat and heads down, he'd let them have the rough edge of his tongue! Someone would have to bale, and that would be risky. The French kept popping away as fast as they could reload. In a moment or two another one — another half dozen! — of the French guard boats would pull up to investigate.

There was absolutely no time to lose.

In the ebb with the current flowing fast the boat was as unhandy a beast to manage as a hungry donkey. Fox kept the bows in the right direction; but that called for herculean effort and immense concentration. The calculations were tricky. They flowed through his mind without the usual zest he found in working out the sums of life and death. On him depended the lives of his men, of Grey and Carker and all the others, and although that was always true — for was he not their captain? — it smote him with redoubled force now.

The bows swung and he smashed at the oar to force the stern around and bring the bows on again. The ebb kept swinging him off line. There was only one way to do this. Deliberately, Fox sculled his boat around, heading the bows inshore of the French boat, heading them up until they centred upon the waterlogged British boat. He was within range and the Frogs hadn't seen him. They were far too busy shooting away at men who couldn't shoot back.

A Frenchman, probably the boat commander, had yelled a demand for a surrender. The reply had made Fox's thin and cruel lips twitch. Grey was learning Foxey ways ...

With a bound like that of a constipated antelope on some Italian mountain crag, Fox leapt forward. He took his oar with him. He plummeted down in the fore-sheets. The bows were swinging. He dug in the oar and thrashed white water away. The boat rolled. Flint and steel. The match took. Why hadn't the snail eating Frogs the sense to put a lock on the gun? He blew on the match, bent over the gun to peer along the line of metal. Coming on ... Coming on ... He could see the bows of the French boat moving across the bows of his own, see the humped black figures there, the reflected flash of a musket ... Now ...

With a satisfied gesture of pure venom, G. A. Fox thrust the lighted match down upon the touch-hole.

Chapter Two

The gun roared with a remarkable display of ferocity for a little two-pounder. The tongue of orange flame blinded everything for moments. Fox tasted the acrid bite of fired gunpowder on his tongue, gritty and exhilarating, and spat.

The noise buffeted his ears and rang in his head. He made two gigantic leaps back in the boat, stumbled and almost fell on something slippery and unnoticed before, reached the sternsheets on his hands and knees, giving himself an infernal crack along the head from the tiller.

Through sparks and noises both inside and outside his skull he grabbed the oar, for the confounded thing had almost spun overside in his lunatic-like antics, and set to sculling up to the boats.

The yells over there had changed to shrieks of agony. He'd shot off a damned sight more than a mere two pounds of old iron. The darkness lit again, fragmentary moments of vivid orange and ruby colorations interspersed with greyer swathings of shadow as smoke drifted across the conflagrations and the ships burned away. In that eerie light he saw the French boat as low in the water as the British, with odd humps and sticks showing above the gunwale. It took Fox, vigorously thrusting his oar at the water, a moment to understand these were the corpses of the crew. Those still alive were frantically baling and yelling. Fox sourly commented that there seemed to be more yelling than baling.

He lifted his own powerful foretop-hailing voice.

"Ahoy! You Nuthouses! Look alive, you bunch of rapscallions! Light along there! I'm coming alongside!"

The sourness in him did not vanish as he wondered just what his men were doing and thinking now; it merely changed direction. Bigod! Didn't they calmly take all the miracles he performed for them as mere matters of course? Of course they did!

Proof of that came as John Carker hailed.

"Aye aye, sir!" followed instantly by: "Keep clear o' the Froggies, sir. They're in a nasty mood."

How easy it would have been to shout back that they were in a mood of sweetness and light compared to the nastiness of the mood in which Commander Fox now was. Easy — and puerile.

Instead, Fox bellowed: "Bring oars with you, Mr. Carker! This boat's short."

"Aye aye, sir."

The French were in a nasty mood.

A musket flamed and cracked and the ball splintered into the transom a handbreadth from Fox. He cursed. Over there the French boat was swinging stodgily now, caught by the ebb and turning. The British made a few attempts to pull; but their boat, also, was too far gone. Fox sculled down, reflecting that the French should have no more muskets or pistols capable of firing by this time. The wetting they'd taken when his freely discharged present of grape and langrage had chopped into the boat's hull and men should — must — have rendered every weapon unfit to fire.

Standing up like this, wearing a white shirt, sculling away, Fox presented a target any musketeer would gloat to see.

There was nothing else for it but to scull on down and trust to whatever fates, whether divine or Lady Luck's, that had so far looked after him in matters of this sort, to continue to confide some protection to his skin.

Shouts and imprecations blasted the night.

Fox let the French get on with that and sculled down on towards his men. They were ready for him. Grey and Carker, at least — and probably all of them — had worked out what their captain had done, and so there was no need for longwinded orders. The hands heaved themselves up, all dripping wet, bundling into the seaworthy boat. Oars were passed across.

Here were Grey and Carker, thumping down into the stern-sheets.

Fox handed his oar to Josephs, who would row stroke, and that large and fearsomely muscled man grunted as his massive hands wrapped about the loom.

"Silence in the boat!" rapped out Fox. He remained standing, balancing easily to the gentle roll of the boat, looking forward at the upturned faces of his men. Mr. Midshipman Eckersley had taken himself off into the bows, and was squeaking away at the hands, telling them in shockingly intemperate language to get their oars settled and ready to stroke, before Fox's order silenced all.

There they were, his men. He saw them all, noticed that some had been wounded, with the blood dark upon the rags swathed about head or shoulder. He counted them, very deliberately. All there. Every last one.

Only then did G.A. Fox sit down and give the order to give way.

Barnabas might cox. Fox felt the end of the night's affair strong upon him, an anti-climax that, in truth, was no anticlimax at all for these men of his. Hadn't they been sinking in a waterlogged boat? Weren't the damned French shooting at them? Weren't the only alternatives being shot to death, drowned or taken up to be a prisoner of war?

And then, out of the fire-shot night, steering his own boat, had sculled their captain, had blown the Frogs to Kingdom come, and taken them aboard, and now, here they were, calmly pulling out from the bay of Point Avenglas, pulling out to the open sea, to the frigates of the English squadron and safety!

Yes, there had been another touch of the old Foxey magic for his crew.

With these maudlin sentiments uppermost in his mind, Fox addressed himself to his two lieutenants. Barnabas stuck stolidly to his tiller; and by a slight forward inclination of his body, Fox could put his head close to the heads of Grey and Carker, opposite, who inclined in a similar manner.

"And, gentlemen," said G. A. Fox with that ferocious grimace like a death's head about his face. "How comes it you are swanning about here when according to my orders you should have been out of the bay by now?"

Grey looked at Carker and Carker looked at Grey.

Fox fixed them both with a steely gimlet from those eyes which had been described as ice floes.

"Well, sir," began Carker, who although serving as a volunteer and second lieutenant to Grey, was the senior of the two by a week. "Well, sir — we ran into a little trouble."

"That's right, sir," said Grey with that easy confidence that could so charm and so irk. "A damned Frog guard boat challenged us and by the time we'd dealt with the pesky feller, why, we'd been stoved and swamped, and —"

20

"And then the other French boat arrived, sir," said Carker, his honest face shadowed and troubled. "We were like to be done for if you hadn't arrived up when you did."

"No, by God!" said Grey. "Trice me up and tar me! But that was as pretty a piece of work as I've ever seen! Devil take me else!"

Fox did not say: "Ha harrum!" in that stupid way some sea officers had. But some comment was called for.

"And I suppose the hands would confirm all this, should I decide to ask 'em, hey?"

"Of course, sir!"

"Most certainly, sir!"

Well.

He knew damned well what they'd done. They'd pulled sufficiently far off that he couldn't see them and then they'd rested on their oars until they'd begun to pull back for him after *Nuthatch* had blown up. The story about the French guard boat was probably true for that could be just about the only explanation for their failure to reach him moments after he'd dived into the water.

Fox's thin lips ricked up at thought of that dive. The dive had turned into an almighty long flight through the air. Blown up on his birthday! By God! That was a story he didn't want circulating in the fleet, bigod!

And he had to remember that it was those two hell-raisers, Lionel Grey with his cut glass voice and dashing handsome looks, and John Carker with his honest, blunt sailorman's face and outlook on life, who had ripped out the fore and main topmasts of *Furieuse* in order to get back to Port Mahon and so play a part in his court martial. He provided miracles for his men, right enough; but his men — officers and hands alike — more than reciprocated in devilish ways only the Navy could fathom — and which Fox prayed never would.

Fox straightened up and leaned back. He knew enough about these two to know they would not relish fulsome batteries of thanks from him. They knew he knew what they had done. Between them, in the cast iron rigidity of naval hierarchy, a word, a sign, a blink would be enough.

Fox said: "I think, gentlemen," and then stopped; for in some unaccountable fashion a damned frog had thickened up his voice. He spat out with a savagery he had not intended: "I think, gentlemen, you have already given me my birthday present."

Both of them, both Grey and Carker, both of the ruffians, had sense enough to say nothing in reply beyond the purely naval and formal: "Aye aye, sir."

To break this constraining silence, Fox said: "I'd be much obliged, Mr. Grey, if you'd kindly go forrard and see to that two-pounder. Get Joachim interested — he'll be like a father with a new baby."

Quite deliberately Fox had spoken in a louder voice, for it would be injurious to discipline for the men to know their officers were whispering together and the hands unable to overhear. At his words he caught a snicker or two from the aft thwarts, and he could guess Barnabas bore a huge grin on his face that, in the instant Fox swung about, should he do so, would vanish to leave Barny Barnabas's face its usual hunk of chewed teak topped by that flaming hair.

Grey went forward where he and Joachim, that reliable and never-flustered German gunner's mate, set about reloading the little gun. Peering ahead Fox could see no signs of interference from any French guard boats, but already they'd pulled past the wrecks of two boats in the water. The British gun vessels and the two frigates had left the bay; the French were still criss-crossing the water, zealously seeking out any last remnants of the British force. They were rather like enthusiastic stable-lads clearing up after the horse had bolted, making ready to slam the stable door.

All that meant was that Fox and his crew could be picked up yet, could be taken and incarcerated in a damned French prison for the rest of the war — those that were left alive, that was.

Carker had kept a good tight grip on his captain's shabby old undress coat, and Grey had kept as tight a clutch upon his captain's abomination of a hat. Fox recalled thrusting the garments at his two officers, there on the quarterdeck of *Nuthatch,* as the flames roared and mounted higher, consuming his command. Well, they'd saved his clothes and he'd put 'em on; his command was gone forever.

The boat pulled for the open sea and the English squadron and Fox regarded his men as they swung smoothly in the time-honoured rhythms of pulling their oars. There was Slattery, their maniac of an American, and there was Wilson, the man with the sharpest eyes in the fleet, a claim that was to be seriously challenged by Landsdowne. There was Abdul, the magnificent black man they'd cap-a-barred from the Turks, and there was Finn, the new acquisition. There was Tredowan, a mountain of muscle, for the moment not coxing. There were the tuneful duo, Tarpy and Taffy, sadly without their seven barrelled musket. And — there was Ben Ferris, as young and chipper and eager as ever. As for Parsons, Fox's servant, his heartfelt whispers of "Ohmegawd !" had enlivened everyone.

The others were there, too, Hart and Clay and Baker and the rest, all his men, men on whose shoulders he could weigh down the heaviest of naval burdens and know they would bear them superbly — with the devil of a lot of grumbling and cursing, of course.

Simpson was not there. Simpson had been flogged around the fleet, and Fox had an outstanding item in his little black book to investigate that matter fully. The captain of

Gorgon should be able to answer a few pointed questions, for Fox could not discuss the matter with the hands.

So the boat pulled away from Point Avenglas and the red glare of the night sky dwindled. The sea got up a trifle and a choppy wave slapped at them; but the men pulled with a will and soon the hoarse hail reached them.

Mr. Midshipman Eckersley shrilled a reply that skated up and down a clear octave.

"Nuthatch!"

How amusing it would be to see the faces of Cloughton and Sandeman and his officers in *Alarm!* That hail from the night telling them that the commander of a fireship had returned must strike with all the ghostly force of an apparition.

Soon they were hooked on to *Alarm's* main chains and Fox could spring up onto her gangway and so, doffing his old hat, make his way past the gaping midshipman on to the quarterdeck.

In only moments he was below, faced by the bulging scarlet features and incredulous eyes of Admiral Cloughton and the calm, yet puzzled scrutiny of Captain Sandeman.

"Alive, young Fox! Devil take it! You're like a damned sea-cat with nine bloody lives!"

Cloughton heaved a huge wheezing cough and collapsed back into his chair, sputtering.

Fox knew the form on occasions such as these.

"May I say, sir, how pleased I am to see you have survived the night's action."

And that wasn't much of a form, either. From this roaring, scarlet and bulging-faced admiral Fox hoped to gain further advancement. For Black Dick to have had his brains spattered all across *Alarm's* quarterdeck by a French roundshot would have done George Abercrombie no good at all.

"Aye, young Fox. And lucky to be alive is the damned truth of it! Dawood reported in you'd gone sadly astray."

Fox was prepared for this. Commander Dawood, taking in the other fireship, *Fired rake,* had gone hell for leather through the boom after *Nuthatch* had been brought up by the incompletely cut timbers. *Nuthatch* had fallen off to starboard. *Firedrake* had gone bald-headed for the hulk, burning splendidly. But the French, as brave as they always were, had grappled the burning fireship and towed her clear.

Fox said: "I compliment Commander Dawood on carrying out his orders, sir. But *Firedrake* was towed off —"

"I know! I know!"

Captain Sandeman, a very quiet man, coughed, and said: "We observed a great quantity of fire and a number of explosions from the direction of the inlet, Captain Fox. We supposed you and your ship to have perished."

Fox told them what had happened, keeping it cool and calm and in the Navy tradition. He was well aware they would understand what he was talking about. They would feel the heat on their faces, the stinging beat of fire beneath their feet, see the flames roaring and twisting. They would sense the French roundshot and grape sleeting in. They would know, as no landlubber ever could, just what it was that Fox had accomplished.

He finished: "The two frigates were burned and blew up, sir. I regret it was not possible for me to have brought them out, as the first plan demanded. I therefore carried out the second plan —"

"You did, Captain Fox? By God! You did!"

There was no question of his inventing the story, for the morrow would bring ample confirmation.

Cloughton glared up from under his eyebrows. His hand clenched around a brandy glass and he took a hefty swallow before he said: "Very well, Captain Fox. Damned good. Two Frog frigates Boney don't have. You write it all up in your report. This'll make fine reading!"

"Aye aye, sir."

That was his dismissal. Now he could go and find that cot and see if Parsons had managed to rustle up a tot of rum from some damned illegal store he'd have access to. Parsons could winkle out rum like no one else. He'd have a tot ready for his captain when they got to Saint Peter's Gates — or to the portals of hell, more likely.

George Abercrombie Fox stretched and felt the tiredness in him like a ball of unravelled wool, fuzzy and soft and betraying.

But, by thunder, it had been a night to remember!

Chapter Three

Whilst it was undeniably pleasant to be able to sit in the chimney corner and stick his feet out into the warmth of a real coal fire, with the Taproom echoing to the cheerful noises of men drinking, swearing, playing cards and yarning over impossible nautical adventures, Fox must still keep reminding himself he was on half-pay, and likely to be on half-pay for some more time.

He was called Captain Fox, although everyone knew he was only a commander and therefore not a *real* captain at all.

He drank black beer sparingly, husbanding his money. He'd elected to stay on at Portsmouth for a spell. He would go back to the old house by the Thames to see his family soon enough. He'd have to go up to London and hang about the Admiralty and that horrendous waiting room, knowing what little hopes he had of finding anyone to give him a ship there.

For the time being his main chance lay with Admiral Cloughton. Black Dick had taken poorly again; but was up and about once more, hawking and spitting and choleric of face and damn-you-to-hell of voice. Fox had visited him at the house in which the admiral was being put up, the home of some distant relative most flustered at having an admiral to stay, and dismayed, to put it no higher, at Black Dick's constant demands for fresh rum and brandy, and his bellowing voice echoing about her delicate rooms.

The problem, of course, was that Cloughton himself was once more unemployed. With the successful action in which Fox had commanded in default of anyone else to give the name of Cloughton lustre, it could not be long before My Lords of the Admiralty requested him to hoist his flag again. Come the day, said Fox. Come the day. He felt certain that Cloughton would be fully sensible of the obligation he owed this right tearaway, this tarpaulin sea officer, this G. A. Fox. When that day came, why, Fox would take a command — might even, given that fate might smile upon him, at last be posted.

There were literally hundreds of bright young men waiting to be posted. There were hundreds of captains on the Navy List, and many of them were never likely to get a ship. These were the pressures and although the Navy was bigger than it had ever been and was growing larger every day, there were very very many men who would never command, would never be posted.

For George Abercrombie to number himself among these failures was something he would not do.

Certainly, one thing remained sure. All this scurrying about he had done, up to Yarmouth, seeing about the *King George* packet, all the squalls and storms, those three distinguished passengers, idiots who would insist on unharnessing horses from the coach and dragging it through the streets of Essex towns, the stiffness and the formalities of the events leading up to Nerot's Hotel, the chariot for Earl Spencer, the disaster of arrangements made in haste and forgotten, the whole frantic episode had to be put out of Fox's mind. He had sworn that to the little man with the one eye and the one arm, the man who was now the Hero of the Hour. One thing was damned sure, Nelson hadn't been blown up on his birthday, which happened to be the same day as Fox's. Nelson had been in Prague, capital of Bohemia, where the Archduke Charles had given a grand party at his palace.

Fox saw through Nelson — saw through the fussy little man with what was so bitterly said of him in the newspapers as being true, but only a tenth of the truth. Nelson was a sailor; of that Fox was as well aware as anyone. My God — hadn't he refused to sail in the Viennese *Bellona* specially sent for him when he couldn't get a British keel, a warship from whose gun deck the guns had been banished except for twenty-four, to be replaced by silk hangings and eighty beds? And hadn't this fine, fancy decorated warship been taken by privateers in the very Gulf of Venice itself? Fox would sail with Nelson if the chance ever came his way again, ever and always.

As it was, Nelson was making the rounds of polite society in London, circles from which a jumped up Thames marsh-boy was excluded, while Fox toasted his feet before a coal fire and hoped for employment.

One odd fact had emerged. Fox had mentioned that he, too, possessed a Star of the Crescent, given in much the same style as Nelson's own, although not of real diamonds, for services rendered to the Porte, the gift of the Grand Signor. Fox had fought at Acre, and had with Chorbaji Murad, a janissary, a chorbaji of the jemaat, taken the three-decker first-rate, the old *Maria*. For these services and others of as unholy a character he had been presented, there on the deserted deck of *Hector,* stripped and ready to go into dry-dock, with the Star of the Order of the Crescent. Fox had taken the distinct impression that Nelson had not known how to receive this intelligence. The Admiral's Fancy, now, even larger and more bounteous, but still a damned handsome woman, had appeared a trifle put out.

Fox knew she had no need to concern herself over any thoughts of rivalry. What? A mere commander attempting to rival the Hero of the Hour, an admiral, the one man in whom all England believed? All England, that was, except the backbiting scandal-mongers, the small-minded lice infesting high society, who stayed at home and grew fat on the profits to be made from the war.

Still and all, George Abercrombie had played cards one evening, and won. He had to be most cautious in card playing, for all his skill at manipulation. He won enough to get the glittering bauble of the Star out of pawn. He didn't dare wear it; but he had taken Nelson's advice and written to Sir Isaac Head at the College of Heralds. No officer might wear a foreign decoration without the consent of the king. Fox might wear his star; but only at functions of the highest heights of dizzy formality. He was scarcely likely to attend any of those; but he was freely permitted to wear the star if ever he visited Turkey or the Levant. At this Fox's thin lips ricked up and he crumpled the thick letter paper, viciously.

He'd give the star and a hundred like it for a warm dry bed, a roof over his head, plenty of grub and brimming pots of rum!

Oh — and a jolly girl or two, of course ...

Many stirring events were taking place in the greater world. Malta — and a damned place that had been to the policies of England in the Mediterranean! — had been blockaded for far too long. Captain Ball had worked wonders with means quite insufficient. But, at last, the final French garrison of La Valetta surrendered on 5th September. Fox read in the papers, the *Morning Chronicle* and the *Morning Post* particularly, that the Russians, whose Tsar claimed some spurious over-lordship of the Knights of Malta, would make trouble. Yet Russia had been an ally; Fox had fought with them. The Russians and the Swedes and the Danes possessed a not inconsiderable number of ships. They had line of battleships that could cause a deal of trouble. They were hard countries, filled with active men at home on the sea — at least, considered Fox, the Swedes and the Danes were, indisputably. He wasn't so sure of the Ruskies.

All this heady atmosphere of great events taking place, of men getting commands and filling their ships with hands that Fox would so desperately need when he was posted, infuriated him with his own impotence. Of what use importuning an Admiralty that turned deaf ears to his pleas for a command?

He kept on trying; he knew he stood little chance.

There were men in the Service who bore him a grudge, as, bigod! he bore them a grudge or two, and they would stand in his light. Men like Captain Stone, Toady Stone. And Captain Lord Lymm, for whom Fox had tried and failed to find any redeeming features. They had Influence and the ears of men who wielded interest. Fox must cling to the shreds of his own interest through Cloughton and, although faintly, through Captain Percy Staunton. As for Lord Kintlesham — well, the old peer's daughter Sophy was the fly in the ointment there.

Pitt and Fox were going at each other like tinker's hammers. That was the Charles James of the Fox ilk, and not George Abercrombie. The Slave Trade exercised everyone's imaginations, with Wilberforce and Clarkson fulminating, and the Planter's Lobby destroying every move. Fox felt so restless he took to striding out against the winter gales, head down, his old hat clapped on firmly, his cloak all ripples and shining rainwater, striding on and on until he could return and so sink dreamlessly into sleep. Even then, a glass or two of brandy had to be forced into action to help.

Over two hundred British merchant vessels were detained in Russian harbours, a riposte by Tsar Paul to England's attitude over Malta, which Bonaparte, having lost the island, had with cunning gamesmanship ceded to Paul. An

31

Armed Confederation of the Northern States threatened to destroy all British hopes for containing France. Sweden, Denmark, Prussia and Russia joined forces to resist Britain upon the oceans of the world. Britain had faced a similar situation before, when the Americans had torn free from their mother country, and had beaten the Armed Neutrality — although America had gone her own way, much to Fox's relief. This time the clouds hovered darker and more ominous than ever.

Now was the time for every ship that could spread canvas and carry guns to be pressed into service, a time when every sea officer should be at sea, serving. And Fox sat mumbling by the fire and stumping about the cliffs, unemployed and damned miserable.

On the first of January, 1801, Horatio Nelson was promoted Vice-Admiral of the Blue.

George Abercrombie Fox remained a mere commander, on half-pay.

Mind you, Nelson would be on half-pay, too ...

Fox wouldn't soon forget the strange gale of wind that lashed London on the day Nelson arrived. Grosvenor Square was pelted by fallen chimney pots. Fleet Street saw tiles whipping off the roofs like papers from the presses. The gale lasted a mere twenty minutes and did a hatful of damage; most odd.

Now he was Vice of the Blue, and with a new flagship, *San Josef,* of immortal fame, being a prize of Saint Vincent, Nelson could look forward to employment, possibly a chance to do great things about this Armed Confederation, and to full pay.

Surely, thought Fox, surely, now, with a fleet being prepared, would see him with employment, also?

He had taken a very cheap room in a lodging house, right under the roof, where he looked after himself. Post captains might take vast retinues of men from their ships; Fox just did not have the wherewithal to pay them, nor the interest to secure their release from the receiving ship. He had to admit that he missed Parsons to look after him. So it was that, as spruce as he could contrive, he walked into the Taproom to read the papers — the Americans after their war with France were in a strange and oddly out-of-sorts mood — and settled down in a corner with the single glass he would allow himself after he had paid to hire the paper.

As a naval officer he must keep abreast of world news. Who knew where he would be sent when he gained his next command? He would not admit the ominous word "if" into his consciousness. The oceans of the world were open to English naval power, and it behoved a sea officer who wished to be considered seriously for employment to know what conditions were likely to be met with.

The Americans had been building fine frigates — George Abercrombie wondered if this Josiah Fox who assisted the master shipwright Joshua Humphreys in the construction of vessels like *United States, Constitution* and *Constellation,* might not be some distant relation — and the Americans had proved themselves and their ships in a few scraps with the French. Tom Truxton, for instance, had underlined the probable power of the US marine for the future by taking *Insurgente* in 1799.

The Algerian and Tripolitanian pirates had picked on merchant vessels flying the new American flag as easy prey, and the United States remained still in a ferment about what best was to be done. British ships carried a pass that allowed them immunity from the Barbary Corsairs; Fox knew well enough that although a little dash was paid to smooth the way, the real backing for these safe conduct passes resided in the power of the Royal Navy.

33

One day, so Fox figured, his booted feet warming comfortably in the glow from the coal fire, one day the Yankee fellows would have to show the Barbary Pirates a touch of the iron fist.

But, of course, all thoughts now turned to the Northern States, and their damned confederation, and what the British government and fleet would do about it.

A group of scarlet coats entered the Taproom, and for a moment a wave of astonished silence swept across the blue coats gathered there. Then, as though a watch had momentarily halted the sweep of its minute hand, and restarted with a jerk, the noise and laughter, the conversations and sounds of heavy drinking resumed. Soldiers! Well, the British soldier was the laughing-stock of the world. Billy Pitt had produced his Quota Men for the Navy, and thereby introduced a few scabs and sores; but Billy Pitt's Army! They'd run from the continent, they'd been carried here and there across the seas, they'd chased an Irish rabble, they'd died like flies in the West Indies — but they'd done nothing at all about planting their regimental flags in triumph over the defeated legions of Bonaparte.

Fox went back to his newspaper.

Presently he heard the lumbering approach of someone across the sawdust, and was vaguely aware of a blue blur in the corner of his eye and the heavy sounding breathing of a man surprised and about to speak.

"Sink me! Captain Fox! By thunder, but it's good to see you again, sir!"

Fox glanced up.

He didn't smile, for that was not his way; but he laid the paper down and stood up.

"Mr. Blane. It is good to see you, sir."

Now, of course, there should follow the offer of some liquid refreshment; but Fox had spent his allowance for the day, apart from a few pennies with which he intended to buy a meat pie later on to sustain him.

This cousin of Jennie Blane's stood looking down on him with the most deuced awkward expression on his features.

"Captain Fox — why, sir, I fancy you look like a man without a ship, damned if I don't." At these words Fox might have struck him; but Blane went rattling on with so artless a display of animal good spirits Fox must perforce simply stand and listen. "May I have the pleasure of ordering you a brandy, sir?" Without waiting Blane turned and bellowed in his sailor's voice and the pewter tankards rattled.

"That is very civil of you, Mr. Blane."

"Civil be damned, sir! Don't I owe you for taking me out of the jaws of the damned Froggies? And, Jennie would never forgive me, else."

Fox swallowed.

"You have news of Jennie, Mr. Blane?"

"News? Aye, if you can call it that."

The potman came over and Blane passed the drink with a gallant air. "Here's for your trouble, my man."

"Thankee, zur."

Fox could guess. He knew. Jack Blane had come into prize money, his agents had paid him out. His ship, *Pike,* a dashing corvette commanded by Commander Purvis, had done well in the matter of prizes on her last commission. Fox knew. He'd been instrumental in bringing some of them in — but not in any way in sharing in the handout.

"Your health, sir, and damnation to Boney."

They drank companionably.

Presently Blane could get down to the real reason he had sought out Commander Fox. Jennie, his cousin with the gorgeous figure and fiery hair and green eyes, and a mouth with the melting properties of a furnace, was in town and had expressed a few thoughts on the subject of G. A. Fox.

35

Fox sighed.

"It's most obliged I am, Mr. Blane. But —"

Even here, in this idle conversation, this appearance of intimacy, he would not call Blane Jack. If Blane dared to address him as George, or as Foxey, Fox would have to stand up and cut him dead. Etiquette demanded these petty things.

"There's an Assembly tomorrow night, sir. It will be a ravishing affair. I know Jennie is going ..."

What to do? He couldn't afford to go throwing his money away again. He'd put all that behind him after that mad spree in Tunbridge Wells. What a sink of iniquity that charming town was! The money he'd spent there! Mind you, he'd been winning it so fast at the tables he'd scarcely heeded the spending of it. But now he lay in the prospect of a command, and that would take every penny he could scrape together. He had made suitable provision for the family, a cross he was proud to bear; but everything now must go to this new command he must be given soon. *Must be!*

"It grieves me, Mr. Blane, to have to tell you I shall be away tomorrow. It is a pity, dammit, but there is nothing else for it."

Blane's open face fell. "Jennie will be deuced disappointed. She'll lead me a hell of a dance."

"Stand from under her lee, then, Mr. Blane."

"Aye!" Blane chuckled, a huge snorting explosion. "Aye! She's like to sink any young scoundrel with a single broadside from those eyes of hers!"

The conversation became desultory. Fox did not offer to buy the next round. He couldn't afford to feel mean over this; a shilling or two might make the difference when his next command needed supplies. It was not petty. G. A. Fox could contemplate giving up paradise for the good of any ship he commanded.

36

But Blane could not stay. Still burbling away about his cousin Jennie he took himself off. Fox stared after him; he still did not know what Interest Blane possessed. It seemed very clear to Fox that another successful cruise in *Pike,* and Jack Blane might well be posted long before Fox — if Fox ever was made post.

Jack Blane paused and exchanged a few words with the potman. This worthy glanced back at Fox, who was just resuming his seat, and then back to Blane as the lieutenant blasted a few choicely vile words. After a moment Blane left. Fox looked at the few drops of brandy at the bottom of the glass — and he damned well did not feel like singing about Spanish Ladies, either — and swilled them down. He placed the glass back on the side-table with so gentle a motion it seemed he was reluctant to let it slip from his fingers.

Jennie Blane was a toothsome morsel, there was no denying that. They'd indulged in a few high-spirited romps together. But, with money so tight, Fox just could not allow himself to be inveigled back into those roaring hell fire ways. Anyway, much though Jennie was luscious, Fox's dark thoughts kept lusting after other charms, thinking of another face that had once been so fat and sweaty and was now so serene and instinct with life and passion. Bigod! But Sophy Kintlesham had turned into a beauty — and even then, G.A.F. had to admit to himself that it was not merely because Sophy had grown into true beauty that he thirsted for her. He had not willingly admitted before that he did. He had only admitted to himself that when, in the Mediterranean, Sophy had been all puppy fat and red and sweaty she had sighed for him and been ready to swoon away for love of her sailor hero, and now that she was an elegant and slim girl of awesome sensuality, she wanted nothing at all to do with that rapscallion ruffian G. A. Fox.

The Duchess of Bowden, she was now. The Melting Duchess.

As he had back in Tunbridge Wells, Fox would not allow that he was in love with Sophy, Her Grace the Duchess of Bowden. Oh, surely, he would marry her like a shot, as she had once planned he should. He'd marry her for the Interest she represented.

As he ducked his head into the bitter rain and trudged along to his fireless and friendless little attic room, George Abercrombie wondered if — now — that was all he would marry Sophy for. If he was given another chance, of course.

He did not take off his old frieze coat. The room struck chill. He sat on the edge of the bed and alternately stuck his hands in his pockets and took them out and blew on them and rubbed them. No, he'd never be given another chance with Sophy. She had been sweet and innocent — and fat and red and sweaty — and she'd thought him the acme of Naval Heroes. Now he was a mere commander with a lop-sided swab, and she was the most gorgeous and perfect Duchess, a virgin still for all she had buried two husbands. One thing was sure. Fox wouldn't be given the chance to become husband number three.

With these reflections coupled with the nagging uncertainty of where his next meal was coming from, and with the desperate hunger for a ship gnawing his vitals, Fox turned in to sleep in little comfort of mind or body.

Chapter Four

There were no letters the next day, which unfortunate circumstance added fresh fuel to the fires of bitterness and moroseness burning within the breast of George Abercrombie Fox. He took a morning stroll on an empty stomach. One decent meal a day was all he would allow himself, making up what he could outside that allowance with a cheap and gristly meat pie. The jug of black ale itself was a good substitute for food.

Staring at the various vessels in differing stages of readiness for sea was rather like sticking a hot knife into his guts. Any one of those ships meant more than any landlubber could imagine, and yet it seemed that landlubbers held iron control of just who should find employment in them.

There had been conversation recently about the fairly new prisoner of war camp, the first ever, opened on 7 April, 1797, called Norman Cross Depot, near a place called Stilton in Huntingdonshire. There were plenty of forts and hulks occupied by French prisoners; Fox wondered if they would be better treated in a proper hutted camp ashore. *Réunion* and *Révolutionnaire* had been the first French warships to contribute prisoners to the camp; by this time there were a lot more. Fox would willingly go out to sea and hunt up a whole cargo of fresh prisoners for Norman Cross Depot, if only their Lordships at the Admiralty gave him the chance.

The rain kept trickling down his neck. Confound it! He'd turn into a certain tavern he knew where cards were played with religious zeal. He'd turn over the cards for a time and he'd win himself the price of a square meal. Any thoughts of using his skill to cheat and thus provide himself with funds to attend the Assembly were immediately thrown out. Fox loathed and detested the sprigs of nobility who, incompetent nincompoops, were found positions of power in ships and led honest sailormen hellish lives. He'd take every last guinea he could from scum like that. But for his peers, the sea officers who manned the king's ships, he held a respect according to their capabilities and characters; he would not cheat them. He was in no case to penetrate into the inner sanctums of the social whirl, for his best uniforms had gone down with *Minion;* so he could consort with his fellow officers and play fair and let his skill bring what might come.

All about him lay a mighty naval machine, the dockyard which fuelled so much of British sea power. For him, Commander Fox, those ships that were the visible representation of that power were like food secreted beyond a glass window to a starving man.

Head down, grumpy, not caring who might be bundled aside from his broad-shouldered bull-like march towards the tavern, Fox blundered on. He heard the click and clatter of horses' hooves and the iron grinding of carriage wheels. The sudden sting of cold rainwater sloshing over him as the wheel dropped into a puddle startled him out of his blind fury into the beginnings of a vicious and obscene tirade directed towards the driver.

"You stupid lollygagging blagskite! Can't you steer a pair of horses, you great clodhopping lump of offal!"

The driver flicked his whip at his offside horse and forbore to reply to the furious face turned up to him. A head poked out from the carriage's drawn curtains over the window. A thin and lean face, vague at the best of times; but quick enough now to recognise this stalwart, chunky, vibratingly furious sea officer.

"God bless my soul! Mr. Fox! I took you to be at sea, my dear sir!"

Fox stood with his mouth hanging open stupidly, like the maw of a shark with the carcase bait abruptly whipped away.

"Lord Kintlesham?" He dashed rainwater from his eyes. "Lord Kintlesham!"

"Of course, of course, my dear Mr. Fox. But, you are wet through, sir! Pray step into my carriage this instant. We'll soon have you roasting before a fire, sir, and a glass of something warm inside you, Good Lord, yes!"

As always, Lord Kintlesham was kindness itself. He carried Fox to the rooms he had rented, elegant, high ceilinged and high windowed, very modern, with much white plaster work about cornice and door frame. The fire roared and chuckled. Lights reflected back cheerfully from mirrors, decanters and glasses. The elegant bronze-footed couch with its red upholstery was very comfortable. Fox warmed himself at the fire and took the drink from the silver tray, the footman most obsequious in breeches and tie-wig, pasty of face, skinny; if Fox had the chance of sweeping him up in a press he'd have that body filled out, those arms muscled, the footman a veritable Jack Tar before they'd been at sea overlong, bigod!

41

Despite his trembling desire to get the conversation on to Sophy Kintlesham, Fox steered clear of her. Let old Kintlesham in his vague, burbling way mention her first.

But Kintlesham was full of the reason for his visit to Portsmouth from his estates in Kent and Sussex. His old face lit with the fires of absolute passion.

"The antiquities, Mr. Fox, are a priceless asset to this country! Why, if the French in their present mood were to have them, Lord knows what would come of it. Those damned revolutionaries simply go around smashing up the past."

"They believe they have good reason," said Fox, cautiously, He was not going to get involved with this man in a political argument. Politics were for politicians. Anyway, with the laws as they now were, with Sedition a very real spectre, no one could really say what they wanted, else they'd be taken up and clapped into gaol.

Mind you, if his brother Archie had his way all the noble lords and ladies would be swinging from handy lamp posts, and the king as well ...

They kept to the subject of the antiquities, and they reminisced over that time in the Mediterranean when Fox, under the nominal command of Mortlock, had rescued Kintlesham and his daughter Sophy with the marble statues, taking them to safety in *Raccoon.* Sophy had been fat and red and sweaty then, and *Raccoon* had been a sweet quarterdeck brig; now Sophy was cool and elegant and the Duchess of Bowden, and *Raccoon* was but a memory, a heap of blackened ashes blown by the winds ...

"And Sophy insists on attending the ball tonight, of course, my dear Mr. Fox."

Well, that was to be expected.

Kintlesham went on, and as he spoke his voice grew both more testy and more resigned, as though his puzzlement had overcome his fretting over his daughter. "I said she was like a painted butterfly, Mr. Fox. And so she is. She doesn't know what she wants — it is all a flutter of preparation and then cancellations. I fancy she plunges into things and then the moment she begins she is bored by them. I tell you, my dear Mr. Fox, I wish she'd made a go of it with you. Damn, sir, I've never known her more happy than in those days in Palermo when — well —" His voice trailed away.

"I regret the information that I was dead ever reached Sophy, but it did, and that is past."

Kintlesham had been staring at Fox's single epaulette worn on his left shoulder, that epaulette which, so Fox swore, contained some bullion. Now the old peer repeated his original observation.

"I must confess I would have thought you to be at sea, Mr. Fox." He leaned forward. "Another glass? This cold weather brings the sweats on a man before he is aware. I drink sparingly as a rule; but winter gets at a man's throat like a wild tiger, believe me."

"Thank you, my lord." Fox stoked up whilst he could. Then, when he answered Kintlesham, there was no way of keeping out of his voice the bitterness he felt.

"I would give everything to be at sea. But I have no ship, I cannot find a ship. Admiral Cloughton — you have heard of him, I feel sure —"

Kintlesham waved a hand, and nodded, and Fox went on.

"The admiral, I feel sure, will not forget me. But he has been unwell and is not fully recovered. Lord Nelson is preparing a fleet — Plymouth, of course — and I can only hope their Lordships will see fit to appoint me. You see, I am a commander and so cannot sail as a lieutenant, although, as God's my witness, if I do not get a ship soon —"

"Come, come, Mr. Fox! Surely life cannot be that bad?"

Well, those were the words one would expect. But Kintlesham was not like other noble lords. For one thing he had been a quiet country gentleman devoted to his antiquarianism, and the fortuitous deaths of relatives alone had thrust him into the position of becoming a lord at all. Even so, even so he had no conception of what it meant to a sea officer to be on the beach on half-pay, no damned idea at all ...

"As I understand it then, Mr. Fox, you must sail as a captain?"

"That is the sum of it." Fox put the glass down with a clatter. He was unsure if that was because his hand was unsteady or because he intended it as a signal. Kintlesham read the message correctly, and the glass was refilled.

"Then this strange habit of wearing a single epaulette has a meaning. I see, I see." Many a landlubber had no idea at all of the vital significance of the epaulette and of its positioning on the left or right shoulder. Suddenly Kintlesham sat up straight. His faded eyes took on a sudden alertness, peering from their tracery of lines, and, for just a moment, all his vagueness and bumbling left him.

"God bless my soul, my dear sir! I see I have been insulting you, sir, and quite unintentionally, quite unintentionally. I confess I know little of these things. But I do know when due respect is to be paid — please forgive me, my dear Captain Fox. I have been much amiss."

Fox laughed.

Incredible. That laugh might sound like the trap of Tyburn Tree opening under a man; but it was a laugh, none the less for that.

"Please do not give it a thought, my lord. The name means a great deal at sea. Ashore —" And here the faded eyes took in Fox's negative gesture with sharp acuity.

"So you are desirous of finding a ship in which you will be captain? I see."

Fox heard the door open at his back; he did not turn his head. Kintlesham looked up and at once his face changed from that reflective look of comprehension of Fox's plight to a new composite of emotions: of love and affection and pity and puzzlement and, most of all, of irritation.

"Ah! Sophy! Come in, my dear. See who it was I found in the street, soaking wet!"

Slowly, slowly, Fox stood up. He turned.

My God!

She was marvellous!

He felt the thump of blood at his heart, the ferocious stab of pain in his loins. He swallowed. He knew he looked the ruffianly boor he was, unkempt, shabbily dressed, his ugly old beakhead of a face lumpy and jutting forward and scowling upon this vision of unutterable beauty — bigod! He was maundering!

The last time Sophy Kintlesham had been in the company of G. A. Fox she had cut him dead, had taken her father's arm and walked him off, the old peer bumbling away and mightily discomfited.

Fox wondered with a flash of barbed cynical pleasure if she would cut him dead in her own household.

Instead, Sophy, her corn-gold hair gleaming in the ruddy glow of the fire, her lissom body full and slim beneath a morning gown of some soft yet clinging stuff, her blue eyes violet in that glow, turned to pick up a book on a table.

"I came for this book, father. I did not wish to disturb you."

She did not look at Fox. Fox wished, now, he had turned as soon as the door opened. He might have seen her face and its reaction as she caught sight of him. He couldn't speak to her.

"Sophy! Here is Captain Fox!"

The moment hung.

All manner of wild Foxey ideas flitted through George Abercrombie's brain. He was not drunk; but he was not sober enough to control the situation. Goddammit! He was drunk — but not drunk with spirits. The sheer sensual allure of this girl scorched him, made him a fool, gave him absolutely no chance. She stood looking at him, perfectly grave, perfectly composed. The high thrust of her breasts beneath the blue ribbon tantalised him, and yet he saw how evenly she breathed, how much of the grand lady she was.

"Captain Fox," said Sophy Kintlesham.

No more.

She said no more.

All Fox could get out was: "Your servant —" and then, he, too, could say no more. He couldn't call her Sophy, and ma'am was hardly right, and as for Your Grace — and here the whole ridiculous situation exploded in G. A. Fox's feverish brain.

He gripped the back of the sofa with a hand so square and so mahogany hard, a hand that could haul a rope or wield a cutlass, he gripped so that the material squeaked. He was about to burst out. He was about to bellow out: "Sophy! You idiot! Stop all this play-acting —"

As he opened his mouth Sophy said: "I trust, Captain Fox, that Mistress Jennie Blane is in good health."

It was like a thirty-two pounder round shot between wind and water.

Fox gaped.

Then: "Jennie Blane? Jennie — confound Jennie! I've neither seen her nor written to her since I saw you last at Tunbridge Wells!"

Sophy's violet blue eyes lingered on his face for a moment. He saw the scarlet flood into her cheeks, and then the whiteness return. The book in her hand trembled.

"I was under the clear apprehension —" she began to say and stopped.

Then Lord Kintlesham burbled: "We were just talking of Palermo, my dear, and —"

"I never think of Palermo, father! It reminds me of Fotherby. I have my book. If you will excuse me."

She was gone.

Fox remembered what followed in the few moments before he took his leave of Kintlesham. Of course he remembered, for did he not possess this wickedly perfect memory? But the whole scene passed in a blur. There were things he must do. He must scrape together every penny he could, borrow against the promise of the future, pester his agents, Snellgrove and Dupre for something at least on account — the courts were taking their usual languid and lackadaisical way with the condemnation of his prizes and their repurchase or sale — get the five-ball sword out of pawn, for that had been presented to him by Lord Kintlesham, badger the tailors to fit him with the best dress uniform that could be managed in the time. The latter he managed by the fortunate chance that an officer whose dress uniform, on order and completed, could never be collected by reason of it lying in fifteen fathoms with a charge of French grapeshot through his guts. Fox felt only the most superficial flicker of regret for the poor devil.

The only way he could ease his supine conscience over this reckless expenditure of money when he was unemployed was to write it down to investment. Investment on two counts. If he cut a fine enough figure he might be invited into those inner rooms where real money was wagered. There he might cheat to his heart's content and take the fat guineas from the fatter purses of the obscenely fat merchants and nobility and grand of the land. And, on the second count, being seen in the society where a sea officer might decently be seen, might assist him in obtaining employment. That was so slender a chance as to be one not worth considering.

But G. A Fox had gone past the rational frame of mind where he would consider the risks and act according to a cunning plan. He marvelled he had not had the courage to do this before. He had tried to scrimp and save; he ought to have splurged on fine clothes and gone sailing down under all canvas and with his guns run out. That was what Foxey would do.

It had taken a slender and gorgeous girl to make him see the stupidities he had been practising. If that was all Sophy did for him, she would have been worthwhile.

And, too, Black Dick Cloughton must find a ship for him soon. The fraternal brotherhood of the Navy was split and sundered in many directions by rivalries and black hatreds, faction against faction, Whig against Tory. Fox had always tried to play politics down the middle of the line. Billy Pitt was in trouble — again — and although no one seriously thought he would leave office, the idea that England might dispose of her ablest Prime Minister in years was not too far beyond consideration.

He paid out again so that his grasping and lantern-jawed landlady grudgingly allowed her half-starved serving wench to climb the stairs with a kettle of hot water. The water cooled palpably, it seemed, as Fox shaved. He shaved carefully. Shaving was a part of life, inseparable from any other part of a sea officer's life; Fox had never been enthusiastic over shaving. Oftentimes a beard would have been a comfort.

His preparations were made. He had arranged to attend the ball this night. The Assembly might shine and glitter away all around him; he would have eyes for one person and one person only.

The ridiculous idea struck him as he went down the steep and cabbagey stairs that he was behaving exactly as a callow youngster smitten for the first time might behave. But — Fox knew enough about his own dark and savage nature to recognise more of the forces impelling him than a callow youngster would even know existed.

His family, employment — these were the mainsprings of his life. What he had to do for his mother and his family he would do, as cheerfully as might be. He might not care over much for himself; might, in fact, loathe the G.A.F. that did these things. That would have absolutely no power to prevent him from doing anything — *anything* — for his family of Foxes.

No — he had dismissed the notion the instant it struck him. No. He would not wear his magnificent although false Star of the Crescent. That would be certain death. Apart from being laughed at and snubbed, wearing the thing would bring down the jealous wrath of every officer in the ballroom without a decoration. The silver medals would be enough to do that — and they would remain in pawn.

The ballroom glittered and gleamed and the music beat out and the candles flickered and people moved neverendingly — in short, the ballroom appeared to Fox like any other ballroom in like circumstances. The very first person he saw as he entered was coughing and spluttering and God-damning away, just inside the entrance.

"Hey! Captain Fox! Just the very feller!"

Admiral Cloughton bore down, took Fox under his lee, and set a course for the nearest alcove seat. On the way he took by boarding a tray of glasses, leaving the plundered waiter staring like a loon.

"Damned nancy-fellers !" Cloughton boomed along. "Ought to be swept up and taught to hand, reef and steer!"

"Aye, sir," said Fox, taking the tray and thus preventing crashing calamity. "But their noble masters will have protections all duly signed and sealed for 'em."

Cloughton was an admiral, and although fond of claiming he had risen solely on merit, possessed Interest. Had he not done so he would not now be an admiral. He was in truth one of the favoured of the land, as Fox was not, and yet Cloughton possessed much of this biting intolerance of the nincompoops who went to sea. He saw in Fox a hard professional officer, to be used hard, to be patted on the head a little in good times and to be severely kicked up the bottom in bad. The odd thing, reflected the gallant admiral, collapsing scarlet and bursting into a chair, was that this Foxey devil never seemed to be in the position of being booted up the backside ...

What Cloughton had to say was said between fits of coughing and spluttering, and between mouthfuls of drink, which went down to join all the other tots in that distended stomach.

"You've seen the *Gazette?* Good. Your name is better known now, young Fox, than ever it was. I've had men ask me about this three-decker of yours. Fox's Patent Boarding Brothel — FPBB they call it. I tell 'em I'd believe anything of you." Cloughton wiped his streaming face. The dance thundered and blared away beyond, the mirrors reflecting the dazzling colours of uniforms, the gowns of the ladies, the lights and the sparkle of it all. Fox kept his eyes peeled.. He paid full attention to the admiral; yet he saw Sophy enter. Sophy looked, so G.A.F. told himself, with a stab, at once sad and uplifting, like a Greek goddess, alluring, sensual, and yet remote and cold and aloof.

"... so Lord Lymm had to have his share of the glory, y'see, Captain Fox?"

"I prefer not to discuss Lord Lymm, sir."

Cloughton glared up out of his pouched eyes,

"You do, do you, bigod!"

"The boom, sir —"

Fox trod dangerous ground here. Lymm, that bastard, a coward and a bully, as Fox knew, had failed. But they were white-washing him. And, because of that, Fox could not expect to receive credit that would discredit Lymm. It was the old story. Cloughton roared on, and Fox paid him attention, and lost Sophy among a swirl of scarlet and blue and gold as the wolf-pack closed in.

"I've made my representations, Captain Fox. Lord Nelson knows my views. I've not been asked to go in any capacity, more's the damned pity. But if any man can do the job it's Nelson, God Bless Him."

"Aye, sir."

Fox's hopes lay shattered.

With Cloughton unemployed, even for a relatively short period, there would be no employment for Fox. That was the way he read the situation, why Cloughton was telling him this, why Black Dick was damning and blinding — and not too genteely, considering the circumstances — and why the admiral was condescending to speak thus with a mere commander.

It was in Fox's way to state the obvious.

"The *Gazette* letter should do you a power of good, Fox. I believe you've had dealings with Lord Saint Vincent already? Well, he's pitched his headquarters at Tor Abbey." Here Cloughton wheezed and choked and then, coming up for air, said: "He and Nelson ain't settled that prize money business yet. Still in the damned lawyers' hands, and they're as civil to each other as ever. A ripe situation."

"Yes, sir."

"Well, young Foxey. You'll want to go and dance now. Get on with it, then. I'll find a little drink and watch. Enjoy yourself, Captain Fox."

And Admiral Cloughton, Black Dick Cloughton, heaved himself up with his stick and a convulsive effort and shambled off, spluttering.

Fox, watching him go, said: "Aye aye, sir."

There went all his hopes.

He was done for now. Cloughton could last for a protracted period of unemployment in comfort. Fox could not. He was done for, damned, finished and on the beach.

Chapter Five

     Captain Kinglake came over to exchange a few words with Fox. Kinglake looked immaculate as always and in the glittering surroundings of the Assembly ball his uniform, his gold lace, everything about him, revealed the young and successful captain thrusting forward confidently in his career, forging his way up the captains' list. Kinglake carried no glass and was not drinking. His ice-cold eyes and his fair hair reminded Fox of past escapades when they had served together, and of the moment when Kinglake, acting for Admiral Cloughton, had told Fox of the spying mission with Etienne to Point Avenglas.

     "You have my sincere congratulations, Captain Fox. I read the letter in the *Gazette* with great interest."

     "Thank you, sir." Fox had himself under control now. He did not wish to run foul of this man's hawse. But he could not refrain from adding: "I was interested in the letter, sir; but I read it with little satisfaction."

     Kinglake regarded him sharply.

"Come now, Captain Fox! You were spoken of in terms of high praise."

Fox favoured Kinglake with that look that could congeal a spluttering linstock match. Kinglake looked away. "I understand, Captain Fox." He spoke in a low voice. "But the admiral had his reasons. It would have been to no one's advantage to have revealed the catastrophe at the boom and the author of that shambles. The work was done, and the frigates burned."

"Yes."

Kinglake changed the subject and, probably without realising it, brought the point of agony directly back to Fox's own dark thoughts.

"Hecuba is ready for sea. I sail to join Lord Nelson — and I need not tell you how heartily glad that makes me! But Admiral Cloughton will not now be sailing with me ...'

"He has just told me —"

"Quite. You are a commander now, and if you will pardon me for saying so, I believe I regret that, for otherwise I would have been most willing to take you as a lieutenant in *Hecuba.*"

Stiffly, formally, feeling as though he would burst asunder with the fury in him, Fox must make a polite reply.

"Thank you, sir. You are most kind."

"It's to be the Baltic. Everyone says so." Kinglake's cold eyes did not reveal his thoughts. "They're a fine spirited people up there, all of them. I'd sooner be fighting the real enemy —"

"Damnation to Boney," said Fox.

"Amen to that, Captain Fox."

Fox knew well enough Kinglake did not mean he was afraid to fight the Danes, or the Swedes, but that he regretted the necessity. Britain's natural enemy, at this time as so often in the war-torn relationship between the two countries, was

France. Jack Corse was the fellow who needed the black eye and the bloody nose, not those countries who had been subverted by Bonaparte.

After a few further minutes of general conversation, dealing with the topics so close to a naval officer's heart, Kinglake excused himself and Fox was free, at last, to seek out Sophy Kintlesham. As was to be expected, the Duchess of Bowden was fully engaged for every dance.

Nearby a group of chattering females, universally fat and ungainly — or so it seemed to Fox in his present state of mind — were exchanging squawks and shrills about Queen Charlotte's tree. Fox could not fail to gather that the queen, German born, had ordered that a yew-tree in a tub be placed in the centre of the room at Queen's Lodge at Windsor. The tree had been hung with fruits and toys, almonds and sweetmeats, and brightened by small wax candles. The sweets and toys were given to the children for whom the party was held.

Well, Fox knew enough to know they would be the children of the high and mighty of the land, the leading families of Windsor, people far removed from the shoeless, ragged urchins of the London stews and the Thames marshes of his boyhood.

Christmas Day 1800 had, it seemed, brought in this event, the Christmas Tree, and Fox wished 'em well of it.

Sophy simply turned her back to him, engaged in an animated conversation with simpering gaggle of admirers.

Her shoulders! Her dress! She looked wonderful — so much so that Fox began to harbour dark suspicions that his interest in her was now far deeper than the interest she would bring to his naval career. He had sworn he would never fall in love. No sea officer could think, if he was sane, of marrying until he had reached post rank. That kind of imbecility was frowned on by their Lordships. No — no, it wouldn't do.

He must resign himself. Sophy meant what she so plainly inferred. Fox was a boor, a lecher, a drunken gambler and the Duchess of Bowden could have no interest in him whatsoever.

Apart from those few heartless words spoken by Sophy — spoken in her sweet musical voice but still cold and hard and heartless — informing him that she was fully engaged for the evening, they had exchanged no other words. Fox turned away. The sight of Sophy's slender form in her gown, the blaze of her shoulders, the fire and glitter of her jewels in tiara and necklace and rings, filled him with a baffled fury. Lust and self-contempt, anger and despair, made him swing away from her as sharply as she turned away from him.

He heard her laughter as she was caught up in that brilliant crowd of buffoons. They were men of the world. They were rich or wealthy, they had prospects and employment and Interest, they were men for whom Sophy could feel an attachment. Just for a moment, just a moment, G. A. Fox considered if he should stalk up to them and, blinding and goddamming to hell, challenge 'em all and so break down the doors of hell and damnation.

Then he saw Jennie Blane.

She came in on the arm of a marine, a captain, stiff and formal and bearing all the hallmarks of pride in his own corps, and, to boot, pride in the beauty on his arm. Jennie saw Fox.

She greeted him with so much surprise that more than a few heads turned to stare. Fox didn't give a damn about silly fat women and silly fat men staring at him. He didn't want to see Jennie now. Mind you, she was voluptuous with her red hair and green eyes and that figure he had seen stark naked ablaze in the candlelight, many and many a time, in Tunbridge Wells.

"Why! I do declare! George!"

"Your servant," said Fox, favouring her with a bow he knew she would understand as a slap in the face.

"George! Jack told me you would not attend the ball! He said —"

She became aware of the greedy eyes sucking in this byplay of bad manners. She caught herself.

Fox said: "I had not intended to come, Jennie. But I unexpectedly met an old friend and was overpersuaded."

That, of course, was a clear and definite insult.

The marine winced. Jennie had dug her claws into his arm.

"Perhaps I shall see you later, George?"

The marine captain, a fine looking man with a scarlet uniform shrunk on to massive shoulders, was glaring at this oafish naval commander with great malice. Suddenly, Fox realised he didn't dislike Jennie Blane. She was a great girl, a fine romp, and she had been kind to him.

"Jennie," he said, and at the tone of his voice she flushed up, painfully. "Jennie — I hope we can meet later — for old times' sake."

At the moment of parting Fox turned, bowing again — and this time his bow carried a very different meaning — and looked after them. His left eye was beginning to admit of a little light, the hazy glow of candles, the dim flicker of silvered reflections. That left eye bore a wound received in some battle of his past and would shut down in purple and black in moments of lust or passion or stress. Well, his left eye had been narrowed and finally stoppered by that infernal ring of pink and purple. The mere sight of Sophy had started the damage, and Jennie had completed it. But, now, he could see a little more clearly. The marine captain and Jennie Blane walked off. There was no sign of Sophy or her ring of admirers, yet Fox felt absolutely sure Sophy had witnessed his encounter with Jennie.

Hadn't she witnessed a scene between him and Jennie, in that gambling den in Tunbridge Wells? Hadn't she stiffened up, deathly pale, turned, scorning even to speak to him, and left him to his cards and his brandy and his banknotes and to Jennie's wanton display?

Well — this time she'd witnessed more of the same, in a different language.

Goddam all women! Give him a ship! A ship with which he could fall in love, a ship in which he could sail and sail, a ship he could call his own — that was all G. A. Fox wanted from life. Plus his regular demands on the bounty of fate, of course ...

The decision to leave this disastrous ball took no effort to make.

He'd have to see about retrieving some, at least, of the money he'd so lavishly laid out.

My God! These women were addling his brains!

Hadn't he decided to worm his way into the inner rooms and there fleece some of these gilded nobility?

Gambling was a disease in wartime Britain. Flour was short and pies and pastries were half-remembered delicacies in most households. Bread was so ruinous a price that a loaf a week was luxury. Beer was thin. Spirits and wine, smuggled from enemy France, cost the earth. But, among the aristos, luxuries still abounded and gracious living was still possible. The fat and wealthy of the land would not starve. And if their womenfolk might not so easily buy silks and satins, they could afford cashmeres from India, and claim the latest silk they wore came from their mother's made-over gowns, instead of being bought from the last pair of hands of the chain that had brought it across the channel last week.

So for a couple of pleasant hours, George Abercrombie fumbled and bumbled in his usual way across the card table, and steadily won, to his expressed surprise. Yes, he was very good, was Abe Fox, when it came to fleecing bastards of nobles who owed him and his kind for a thousand years of servitude.

Mind you, if Fox managed to get himself posted, and then contrived to fight a really successful action, he could find himself lifted into the ranks of these high and mighty. Even then, though, he fancied he'd be a foul and useless noble. He'd not give a damn for another man if that meant depriving his own family of Foxes; but enough would suffice. He couldn't see himself grinding down the poor workers as a matter of course. Just as he would steal everything from a man if by that means his family might survive, so he couldn't see himself stealing from the poor folk of his youth as these bastards did merely to engorge their already gorged appetites.

And if his thoughts were confused, then was there any wonder at that?

Fox had often considered that if, by some awful chance, he had happened to be a tailor, he would have had to think long and carefully on what he would do about these gentlemen's endearing habit of regarding their tailors as men to whom payment need never be made. He'd kowtow for his family; never for himself. Had he been a tailor, and Lord Lymm treated him as it was known he treated the tailor who was obsequiously glad to outfit him — why, Fox might then stick an iron-hard fist into Lymm's face.

Trouble was, a tailor did not have the fist of a sailor ...

Fox lowered the glass.

He'd been supping too long and too generously.

Damn Sophy!

And damn Jenny!

All he wanted was a ship, bigod, just a keel under him ...

The candle light made his eyes ache. He did not have a headache. George Abercrombie was capable of drinking most men under the table, a gift of which he was not always proud, and so he stood up, somewhat jerkily, and bid the company good night. He took with him a fair old slice of their purses.

Scarlet flushed, angry, belligerent faces glared up at him as he rose to his feet. These men could be dangerous. He might not have escaped so easily had he not chosen his moment well.

"Sit down, captain!" bellowed a Yeomanry major, all gold and scarlet and pale blue. "We want our chance to win our money back!"

"Aye," said one or two others. "You played deucedly badly, Captain Fox, and Lady Luck must desert you soon."

The moment Fox had chosen, knowing he was running close to the end of his time, coincided with the entrance of Lord Kintlesham. The amiable peer looked about the room for a moment, bewildered, quite unaccustomed to the full-blooded gambling spirit reigning here. Flushed cheeks, too bright eyes, unsteady hands, brandy bottles rolling empty under the table —

"Ah, Captain Fox!" said Kintlesham. "I am pleased, my dear sir, to observe you are leaving, for I have a pressing matter to discuss."

"Your servant, gentlemen," cried Fox. "I'll give you your revenge some other time."

He did not quite venture to take Kintlesham's arm; but he conveyed as he left his reluctance to go and his going was only at the call of duty and a noble lord.

There was, of course, more than one noble lord sitting at the table. Fox was pleased to think their purses were lighter by exactly the same amounts as weighed down his own.

"I fear to see, my dear Captain Fox," said Kintlesham, leading out, "that you frequent — ah — dangerous company."

Fox contrived to appear all contrition.

"You wished to speak to me, my lord?"

"Yes, yes. Although, I confess, my thoughts run to Sophy. She leads me a mortal hard life, Captain Fox. I do not know what I shall do with the baggage — what I can do."

There was nothing, in decency, Fox could say to that.

Life took strange ups and downs. Yesterday he had been sitting shivering in his miserable attic room, and today he was dressed up in a fancy new uniform, with a purse comfortably full, talking intimately with a peer of the realm. Strange ...

Itching though he was to hear what Kintlesham had to say, for the old peer had nothing new to tell him of Sophy, Fox kept the conversation neutral. They settled in a far corner, away from the excitement, where Kintlesham could rest his legs. Long used to clambering over ancient sites in the best tradition of English antiquarianism, Kintlesham found these late night balls a sore trial. He did not drink, and Fox felt an amused stab of relief that he was relieved of that problem. He really had a large cargo aboard tonight.

" ... and Admiral Curtis was able to be gracious, my dear Captain Fox."

Fox concentrated his wandering attention. He had been looking for Sophy among the glittering throng of dancers.

"Admiral Curtis — why, is he not the man who took *Fortuna* and made himself a fortune?"

Lord Kintlesham's thin face, worried and vague as ever, cracked what might have been a smile. "Yes. He fell into a fortune as I fell into a peerage. No matter. There is a Captain Gollon who fell, also." And here Kintlesham emitted a sound somewhat after a Sicilian donkey braying. Fox let his thin lips curl up a fraction, just to keep the noble old duffer company.

But, despite Kintlesham's title, Fox couldn't really think of him as an old duffer. The peer had never shown other than kindness to Fox, amazing though that might be to Fox himself. Sophy, of course, lay at the bottom of that. Kintlesham went on speaking, and as Fox listened he realised that he could never regard the noble lord as a duffer.

"You know, of course, of my friendship with Sir William. We are antiquarians, both — and antiquities, too, in our own right." Again that donkey brayed. For all his worries over Sophy, Kintlesham was in high good fettle. "He remembered you, my dear Captain, and spoke to his good lady." Kintlesham was too much the gentleman to go into all the details, his sense of tact too strong for that. But Fox gathered that the Admiral's Fancy had deigned to speak — or, rather, to write, for the Admiral was locked aboard his flagship in the Sound — and, hey presto! Captain Gollon had fallen down a hatchway and so *Alkon* swung to her moorings without a commander.

At this point Fox felt his heart beating.

"She is, I am informed, armed en flute, although I am nowhere near sure what that may mean."

Armed en flute!

Goddammit!

Somewhat heavily, Fox said: "It means her guns have been taken out of her gun deck. Her ports gape like a row of empty holes in a flute, and that is why —"

"I see, I see!" cried Kintlesham. "A capital notion! I am told she is loaded with stores and is vitally important and not a moment may be lost."

Fox understood that there had been a deal of po' chaise work, and special riders belting hell for leather through the night to accomplish this. Probably one of Kintlesham's grooms had used the good turnpikes all the way, for the country roads were impassable at this time of year.

"I do not know how to thank you, my lord —"

"Tush, my dear Captain Fox! Did you not bring off a quantity of my best marbles — why, poor Sir William lost a very great deal when *Colossus* went down — a terrible tragedy, for his collection is justifiably renowned."

"So I have heard."

"But, mark me this, Captain Fox. Sophy does not know of this and I would not want her troubled by it now."

It was on Fox's tongue to blurt out that no doubt The Duchess of Bowden wouldn't care tuppence for a mongrely swampboy masquerading as a commander. But he refrained. All this holding in his tongue and his natural instincts was making him feel as emotionally bloated as Cloughton was physically bloated. *Alkon!*

So she was armed en flute, with only her quarterdeck and forecastle guns. Well, even en flute a ship would be expected to bear some part in an action if a French privateer attempted to molest the convoy. There might yet be great things to be made from this. But he was not to be posted. Although called Captain he remained still a commander, with his swab on his left shoulder, not a *real* captain at all.

"I suggest, Captain Fox, that you would do well to take up this appointment, for the admiral wondered if you would accept. Your orders are being written, you should have them in the morning."

"Yes, my lord." In the morning he would be a captain in his own ship! Bigod! Incredible, the way of the world.

Chapter Six

"Hereof nor you nor any man of ye may fail as you will answer the contrary at your peril."

A respectful silence fell as Commander George Abercrombie Fox ceased speaking.

The day struck chill although an overcast and wintry sun struggled to break through, and the little cresting waves glimmered dully like pewter. Gulls screeched and racketed; only a few. Their brothers were well inland seeking winter scraps far away from the grey sea.

The whole scene quickened with activity, the dockyard, the harbour works, the town, the many ships with yards crossed and the inevitable carpet of small boats eternally criss-crossing. Fox savoured the whole gorgeous picture, and in that moment as he finished reading himself in, he didn't give a damn that *Alkon* was armed en flute, with only quarterdeck and forecastle guns left to her. She was a real ship and she was alive. The very first words he had read sprang out at him again from the thick official paper: "You are hereby required and directed to proceed on board *Alkon* and there take upon yourself the Charge and Command of the said vessel ..."

Mr. Rattray, the master, clapped his hat back on again, and at this signal Fox said, in his mildest tone: "Carry on, gentlemen."

He turned to Mr. Colledge, the first lieutenant.

"Pray step down into my cabin, Mr. Colledge. Mr. Rattray, would you give me the pleasure of your company. We can take a glass together."

Well, this was infatuated nonsense, to be sure; Fox had to size up the qualities not only of his sailing master and his first lieutenant, but the whole crew, the officers and the hands, and he must do it quickly. His orders called for him to sail with the tide and join Captain Fraser, *Jubilee,* thirty-two, commanding the convoy.

In the great cabin with its array of stern windows — bigod! How marvellous ! A real great cabin that was all his own, at last! Old, *Alkon* might be, practically falling to pieces, shot up and teredoed and rebuilt over and over; she was still a fine ship and she'd serve well. As Salvation, his new servant, set out what Fox referred to as his best glasses — a cheap lot bought in a hurry along with everything else that had been done head-over-heels for this commission — Fox studied Rattray and Colledge.

Rattray, with his silver hair, his bulbous red-veined nose, his quiet and neat uniform, would be sixty if he was a day, a man devoted to his ship and a man who would never hazard his vessel even if the Archangel Gabriel promised him a channel was secure and Rattray harboured doubts. The master was a man perfectly representing the reasons why England's ships coursed the seas with as much safety as they did, with shipwreck touching them only in moments when no man's hand or brain could deny the power of the elements or of chance.

Fox was not as sure of Colledge. He was past middle-age, older than Fox, sullen — hardly because he thought he would inherit his captain's command. Men of Colledge's stamp manned the ships of England. They did what they were told. They looked for nothing beyond the confines of the wooden hull. Fox, himself, might so easily have been numbered among them had not his youthful spirit been fired, had he not realised that the only safety in an insecure life lay in constant attack on life. That, and Captain Sir Cuthbert Rowlands, to whom Fox owed more, even, than he suspected ...

Colledge would go on a spree ashore, and spend his money, and roar and rampage; but he'd come trotting back to his ship quite unable to face life ashore. If he went on half-pay for too long it would kill him.

"Now, gentlemen," said Fox. We have much to do and no damn time to do it in."

Colledge greeted this with a slow swallow, and a thoughtful frown. *Alkon* had been ready to sail when Captain Gollon fell down the hatchway, and it was clear to Fox that Colledge could see nothing further needed to be done. Fox would have to drum some of the sense of urgency and discipline into these people whom he regarded as prerequisites in any ship he commanded.

Why was Colledge sullen?

"We have had our teeth drawn," said Fox. "But we are left with a few fangs. If Jack Corse gets across our hawse we'll sink what fangs we have in his rump, mark my words."

The master nodded slowly at this, and drank, and evidently considered that was his sole and useful contribution to the conversation.

The first lieutenant, a stout, bulky man, with a face that one felt should be florid and instead saw with something of a shock was greyish and greenish and nettled with lines, said something about the unfortunate accident to Captain Gollon and then trailed away. Fox stared at him. My God! Had he been lumbered with a cargo of blockheads? Well, if they were blockheads now, by the time he joined up with the Baltic fleet they'd be sharper. Yes, said G. A. Fox to himself with some savage determination, he'd serve 'em with gunpowder and make 'em sit up sharpish!

"Would you care to inspect the ship, sir?"

Colledge must have put everything into apple-pie order, Fox, with a touch of devilry he recognised as a luxurious resistance to temptation, said: "Shortly, Mr. Colledge. Would you kindly pass the word for Mr. Bembridge and Mr. Fowley to come to the captain's cabin?"

Bembridge was the second and Fowley the third of the ship.

They were his watch-keeping officers, along with Colledge, for *Alkon* was not large or important enough to be able to afford her first lieutenant the luxury and privilege of not keeping a watch. There were the master's mates, of course, who would walk the quarterdeck. As for midshipmen, once again Fox was light in that department, and for once was only partially annoyed. Midshipmen had their place in the scheme of things; he always found himself intolerant of them and their antics and yet overindulgent to them the moment anything of importance happened. They were so damned young ...

Bembridge and Fowley came in and Fox sized them up as the civilities were gone through. Bembridge looked — unfortunately — as though he might be rather too stupid for Fox's tastes. Large and red-faced and much given to god-damning and blinding, Bembridge offered only a body to stand a watch and a voice to bellow the hands to orders.

Fowley looked more promising. Only recently made, he was barely twenty-two, well-built and with an open air look about him that owed nothing to the sea. He was probably as poor as a church mouse, without Interest, and came from a family in Portsmouth who had been sailors for generations past and who had cousins and relations and what not in all the fleets England kept afloat.

Fox did not detain them too long; but he managed to turn the conversation into channels where he might learn all the multifarious things he had to know. Somehow he gained the impression that all of them — including Fowley — were more than a little affronted by that single epaulette aswing his left shoulder.

They felt, Fox sensed, that they should be commanded by a real captain.

Well, damn 'em all, said Fox. *Alkon* was only a flute, a ship whose guns had been removed so that her main deck might be crammed with stores. She would not be manned to full naval establishment, and although every ship was undermanned, this flute was unnaturally short of complement. Fox swore he'd not only sail her; but fight her as well, if need be.

He finally indicated he would make his tour of inspection.

The first thing he noticed, the thing that had struck him when the crew had assembled in the waist to hear him read himself in, was that repetition of the age groupings of the officers in the men. The crew consisted in the main of old men and boys. Prime seamen would be sent to ships that were going to fight.

It was useless to rage. Admiral Cloughton had indicated he was going on half-pay and could do no more for Fox. The chance of *Alkon* could not be missed. It was this ancient flute or nothing.

Fox went everywhere. Colledge had seen to it that the hands had cleared up, and licks of new paint here and there told of horrors hidden beneath. There was no time to investigate every such piece of obscurantism; but Fox quite deliberately prodded his knife into one suspicious smear of new paint, to find the knife sink in with stomach churning ease.

"Mr. Weston!" He rounded on the carpenter, a stolid man with years of experience behind him. "You will see to this at once! Rip the whole rotten piece out!" Fox could have gone on. He could have told the carpenter exactly what to do and how to do it — Fox could have done it himself if necessary. But he reined his intemperate nature in. He'd let Mr. Weston get on with it and then check the results. God help the carpenter if the job was not done properly, for G.A.F. most certainly would not.

He prowled on. He deliberately overlooked a mess kid left where it should not be left. The old hands would try that one on a new commanding officer. No one would own the kid, its incised names and numbers would have been removed. By his reactions to that deliberately abandoned kid the men could go some way to judging the temper of their new captain. Some captains Fox had known had flown into rages, and ordered all kinds of obscene orders; orders that could never be carried out. The ship's corporal and the master-at-arms alone might suffer. Fox wanted to be sure of them before he struck.

As he went through the ship he found nothing of that effervescent joy he had experienced when he'd taken up command of *Minion*. He had felt as though he'd been walking on clouds then. Then he had been up and coming, able to look forward to certain action despite the shortcomings of the gun vessel.

Now, now George Abercrombie Fox had been fobbed off with a mere storeship, destined to act in support of the fleet, to victual Nelson's ships, not to stand in the line with them in the forthcoming battles.

For all this damned sour melancholia of his mood G. A. Fox was never a man to miss an opportunity. Here he must know every stick and timber of his ship, every gun, every store, every mast and scrap of canvas — yes, that was true. But, perhaps of even more importance, he must know the qualities of his men, gauge their temper, judiciously determine if Captain Gollon had quartered the hands so as to achieve the best possible results

Fox would not alter the quarter bill yet. He would not wish to disturb what he knew from experience had been so carefully worked out, and, moreover, worked out with information of the men he did not yet have. Later, when he had seen these new hands of his performing their duty, why, then he might and probably would make alterations.

Back in his cabin where the few trifles he had managed to secure before embarking merely emphasised their scantiness in this cabin, he ruefully realised that what had served him in the cramped quarters in *Minion* or *Nuthatch* would not serve now. Then, with a few goddamns and blindings of his own, he realised he would have to make do with what he had. They were sailing off to war, to show those countries who had succumbed to the iron hand of Boney that old England still carried on the war, and meant to have Boney served up, triced and tarred before breakfast.

There was a growing war weariness in England these days.

Clear it was, and frightening to a naval officer. The war had dragged on since 1793, and nothing seemed able to stop it. England had gained colonies, and her trade increased vigorously. But she was being bled white. The costs of supporting the war were enormous. No wonder people fretted and sought means of seeking an honourable peace. Fox wondered, with much of that insular British cynicism, just how honourable the Corsican bandit could ever be.

Other problems weighed heavily on the temper of Englishmen at this time. Billy Pitt might have had the Slave Trade question taken from under his feet; but he was

70

determined on facing up to the Irish question. The Union was now a fact; but Pitt's desires to make the Union worthy by relieving Roman Catholics of their disabilities and even of granting the Roman Catholic clergy maintenance, seemed bound to fail in the face of that stupid, bigoted and typical opposition that Fox had so often run into headlong, those nincompoops who took all for themselves and would grant nothing to people not of their own.

When Lieutenant Colledge came down to report all was ready to weigh and sail, Fox nodded.

"I'll come up, Mr. Colledge."

He made no reference to anyone other than himself taking the ship out. Truth to tell, Fox fancied the mental exercise of conning *Alkon* out. The sheer pleasure of doing that simple thing — or not so simple, given the general conditions of busy traffic of Spithead — would soothe his mind and perhaps drive away the dark thoughts troubling him.

Damn Sophy, anyway!

Alkon sailed as though she carried a hundred extra tons of granite slung in chains from her keel. Fox cracked his orders out and made no attempt at conversation. Mr. Rattray carried out everything he did with the kind of old world grace Fox associated with butlers buttling for nabobs. *Alkon* cleared her wind and the top-gallants were set and then, in a nice quartering breeze and with the weather looking far less ominous than earlier in the day, Fox set his courses. *Alkon* began to pitch — not too much, enough so as not to alarm or cause Fox to hand the courses. He stayed on his quarterdeck and his face bore an expression that boded ill for anyone foolish enough to address him without a most pressing reason. That old devil's face: that was how his shipmates of former years had described the evil and vicious look that could drop across his features when he was troubled.

Making his number with Captain Fraser whose *Jubilee* hung up to windward of the convoy — a mere six vessels, three flutes like *Alkon*, the other three hired country vessels — Fox slotted his new command into the directed position within the convoy. Sight of the three other flutes came as an unwelcome visitation of the truth. This convoy, small, would be well enough protected by *Jubilee*. A sloop might normally take a convoy of this nature to the other side of the world, if needs be.

The routine of the vessel continued, and Fox kept his usual sharp lookout. Everything that happened aboard contributed to his understanding of his command. He knew and dismissed the dangers that he would be resented. It was natural for a crew to resent a new captain. That was human nature.

Down Channel lay Plymouth and the fleet. In all probability Nelson had already sailed, although Fox fancied they'd have the devil of a rush. They'd probably stop off at Yarmouth before sailing for the Baltic. That would make sense. As his vessel sailed to the larboard quarter of the convoy he could not help wondering if the service might not be better improved if *Jubilee's* orders took her direct to Yarmouth.

He had spoken to no one regarding his new command or of Nelson — or Sir Hyde Parker, come to that — and he knew only that he would take his orders from Captain Fraser. Fraser must have orders to take the convoy under his command, and no doubt Gollon would have known why they were sailing down Channel to attack somewhere in the Baltic. The night wore on and Fox did not sleep. He could not ask his first lieutenant or the master. He felt strongly on such matters. If only — but he had just assumed — the ludicrousness of the situation struck him as a personal affront. He had been given his orders to take command of this vessel and to exercise the utmost despatch in joining Fraser. From now on he was merely a unit of a greater whole. *Had* Gollon known where the convoy was heading? It had to be Plymouth, on this course. Fox fretted.

Damned nincompoops again, sending them chasing down to Plymouth just so they could sail all the way back. Mind you, the wind had backed considerably and a fair old easterner was pushing them down Channel splendidly. They'd have to be careful entering Plymouth.

Fox had sailed under sealed orders before this; but this occasion was different. The itchy feeling that everyone else in the ship knew where they were going and that he, their captain, did not, irked him intolerably.

Well, he just wouldn't sit and be itched or irked any longer. There was a man aboard who would know, a man, moreover, who, knowing, might not vouchsafe that information. These clever people, spies like Roland and Etienne, flag-captains, secret agents of navy and army, were a damned close-mouthed set.

Fox bawled a blasphemous order to the quartermaster as a leech riffled and ruffled and the response at the wheel was commendably quick. *Alkon* had to be kept on station, and inattention at the wheel could have them running their bowsprit into their neighbour's taffrail in short order.

The man he wanted stood by the lee rail, his hands clenched up into the small of his back under the massive cloak he wore tightly fastened. Despite the muffling cloak there was no mistaking the military set of the shoulders or the height and power of the man. Fox did not generally care for passengers; this time he would turn the trick to his own advantage.

With his cut glass voice under perfect control, Fox said: "It's a chilly night, major. Would you do me the honour of taking a glass?"

The man started, as though his thoughts had been miles away.

He turned and Fox saw more clearly than he had before the broad full face, the skin strangely smooth and shaven where one might expect the cragginess of a frontiersman.

"With great pleasure, sir." The major half inclined his head as he spoke, overtopping Fox by a ridiculous amount. His voice carried that familiar and, to Fox, nostalgic drawl of the Canadian. Fox recalled his days as a powder monkey in America. He'd met Canadians then — and since — and he admired them for the toughness of their lives and the way they'd fought. This man held himself well, and carried all the limber strength of those men Fox remembered so well.

The supple strength of Major John Mansfield was further revealed to Fox in his cabin as the grey cloak was removed to reveal the blue silver-frogged jacket of the light dragoon. Mansfield wore regulation white kerseymere breeches buttoned below the knee. He had had the sense to remove his steel spurs from his black leather boots. Fox nodded as Salvation brought in the pewter tray and the thick glasses.

"Rum, major, is what I fancy it most politic to offer. I had no time to outfit with wine before we sailed."

"Rum," said Major John Mansfield, with a smile, "will suit admirably, captain."

As Fox had suspected, this Canadian major of light dragoons was a tough nut. No sense in beating about in a foul wind; just put up his helm and steer for board and board, bash straight in the old Foxey way.

"You have experience of the Baltic, major?"

Mansfield lowered his glass — he had taken a hefty swallow and Fox expected to be busy having the Canadian's glass refilled — and a puzzled expression accompanied his reply.

"The Baltic, sir? No — I know little of it. I am glad to think that Lord Nelson has been given employment."

Fox drank a little more quickly than he intended.

"Your services will no doubt be required ashore — you speak Swedish, Danish, perhaps?"

Mansfield, still a little puzzled, smiled again and drank and Salvation refilled the glass. Fox turned his ugly face towards his new servant. "I'll see to that, Salvation."

"Aye aye, sir." Salvation retired.

"Why no, sir. I understand not one word of the languages. Nor Russian, either. I have a fair to middling grasp of Castilian — of course, French, well —" He shrugged. He'd be bilingual from the word go there, Fox knew. Mansfield went on: "I am taking passage to the Levant because I have some fluency in Arabic, Captain Fox —"

Fox was gaping.

Fox was stunned.

"The Levant?" he bellowed. But we're going to —" And then he got a grip on himself. Mansfield was looking at him in the most curious way. Fox swallowed.

"You speak Arabic, major," he heard himself say, in a voice like an echo from a lead lined coffin.

"Yes. Business took me to the Levant at an early age — long before the war. My father —" He hesitated, and clearly changed what he was going to say. "It was felt my attachment to the Corps of Guides would be advantageous, and General Abercromby most kindly asked for me. We are —"

"General Abercromby!"

Fox forced his rigidly constricted hand to relax upon the rum glass. He knew he wore an idiotic death's head grin upon that lumpish figurehead of his.

Where were his dreams of sailing with Nelson? Where his schemes to get into the battle that Nelson was surely going to find? Where his plans for that glorious and profitable future with the fleet whose commander and officers filled the eyes of everyone back in old England?

The Levant! Acre and Alexandria and Turkey and the stinks and flies and diseases and sand — Bigod!

He'd been cheated again!

75

George Abercrombie Fox had once again been sent off on a fool's errand to an army that swanned about the Med doing nothing. When all his desires and enthusiasms urged him towards the north, he was being despatched ignominiously to the south.

Goddam that jezebel fate who treated him so!

Chapter Seven

Two months was the normal time a normal man would allot for a voyage to the Levant. Captain Fraser had his orders and they included the repetitive command to make all the haste possible commensurate with safety. Gibraltar came and went without a single hitch, the Gut being traversed by an uncommonly kind westerly. Into the Mediterranean.

Into the Mediterranean — again!

Fox looked at the sea, darkly blue and quite different from the chill grey waters of the Atlantic. Lord! What times he'd spent in this inland sea! He thought of *Raccoon* and then would think no more of those past passages in his turbulent life.

His acquaintanceship with Major John Mansfield had ripened into an association that Fox, a man for whom friends could be numbered on one finger, hesitated to call friendship. Fox had never dared to admit openly that Lionel Grey and John Carker were friends. Their association was at once too intimate and too fragile to be troubled by clumsy attempts at labelling.

But for a true friend outside the family, Fox could think of only one man, Rupert Colburn of the Forty Third.

He wondered if Rupert had been successful in buying his majority, and hoped he had. Rupert looked out for Bert, one of Fox's younger brothers. They'd been out in the West Indies for a hell of a time now, and Fox, whenever he thought of them, sent up a mental prayer that the black vomit would not take off his brother Bert and his friend Rupert Colburn. Stationed at Saint Pierre, they had seen their whack of action. There had been rumours, so Rupert had written in the letter in which he'd mentioned his chances of promotion, that the Forty Third, the Monmouthshire Regiment of Foot, might be returning home in 1801. If they did, and Fox was stuck away in the Med, and they were sent on one of these nonsensical expeditions dreamed up by the Horse Guards — and he never saw them!

Quite automatically, swaying with the heel of the constant onward passage of *Alkon,* Fox bellowed a fierce order at the quartermaster.

"Steer small, damn you!"

"Aye aye, sir."

Alkon kept on forereaching the other vessels in convoy. Well, that meant a deal of backing and filling the mizzen topsail; but Fox didn't mind that. He'd been thrashing this crew into something like the order he demanded. But that steady onward speeding of *Alkon* pleased him. At the first opportunity he'd redistributed the weights. That had meant a deal of cursing effort as the hands shifted the stores. But he'd done it.

Generally speaking the best point of balance for a ship, the centre of gravity, was a little forward of the middle point. Also, as Fox well knew, a ship needed to be fine in her after lines, so as more easily to allow the water to run clear. But in an oldish ship like *Alkon,* built on rather stubby lines, the best positions could only be found by compromise. Fox achieved that very necessary leanness of her flanks by lifting the stern a little more than usual, accepting the extra obstruction of the bluff bows, finding the compensations gave him a clear extra knot.

He felt supremely confident that if he set all his canvas he could outrun any ship of the convoy — aye, and make *Jubilee* set her studding-sails to keep him in sight. *Alkon* might not have new copper; but she had been freshly breamed and was clean as a whistle beneath.

They spoke not a single sail.

The weather began to give a hint of what the Mediterranean could do in summer, and the westerlies stayed with them. It was far too early in the year for a Levanter, and Fox expected a quick clear run. Well, if he was to be employed as the captain of a storeship dancing attendance upon an army that had achieved nothing, instead of sailing with Nelson to glory and prize money, then, bigod, that was what he would do.

He had dined with Captain Fraser, and been fully informed of his orders. They did not amuse him. When Fraser finished, Fox could not refrain from saying: "All this could have been achieved bloodlessly in 1799, sir."

Fraser, a thick-bodied, swag-bellied Scotsman with a high colour and a high opinion of himself and a high hand, fleered a cold fish look upon this tarpaulin commander.

"You refer, of course, to the Convention of El Arish?"

"I do, sir. I have had the honour to serve under Sir Sidney Smith and from what one hears of his dealings with Kléber in Egypt —"

"He had no authority to negotiate."

Fox realised he must tread warily. Sidney Smith had arranged a convention whereby the French Army in Egypt, abandoned by Bonaparte, might with honour be returned to France. This would not only have given immediate control of Egypt to England without a drop of blood being spilt, it would also have landed in Metropolitan France an army of veteran soldiers who were much incensed with Bonaparte's betrayal of them. The coup of Brumaire might have been reversed. These things could easily happen in a country as torn with strife and civil commotions as France after the Revolution.

In the event the British Government, willing to ratify the convention, had been unable to do so because of lack of information of Lord Keith's reaction — with Nelson's — to the idea of allowing French soldiers to escape scot free. It might still have been possible; the Turks, who had been beaten time and again by the French Army, were only too happy to have Sir Sidney make the arrangements. But a fanatic called Souliman-el-Alepi had assassinated Kléber, striking him down with a dagger as he walked along the terrace from the house of General Damas, where he had breakfasted, to the headquarters.

Kléber, an efficient and distinguished general, had been succeeded by the jackass General Menou. The whole French Army had been driven into high spirited mirth at Menou's adoption of Islam, and the fool called himself Abd-Allah Menou.

He had refused to have anything to do with a convention.

Souliman-el-Alepi had been twenty-four years of age. He had been by profession a writer. Dangerous men, these writers, considered Fox. Although he doubted if Wordy or Sam or Godwin would strike down an enemy general with a dagger, they would do that, aye, and worse! with their quills.

So now General Abercromby, an old general and one well-liked in the army, had been ordered to descend on Egypt and defeat the veteran French Army. Fox pondered. The British Army was at about its lowest mark for years. Its morale was suspect, for it had suffered reverse after reverse. It had tried to do all manner of things, sending penny packets of soldiers here and there, and had failed everywhere. Fox himself had

80

participated in one such futile landing. Now contingents of the army had been swanning around in the Med and the Atlantic, threatening to take Cadiz, threatening to descend here, there and everywhere, and in actuality doing nothing except make the men seasick.

Against Bonaparte's veterans, men who had stormed to victory across a hundred battlefields, what would the redcoats do, landing in the face of hostile fire?

The supplies he carried in his flute now made sense, for they were mostly army stores.

"The army badly needs the supplies we carry, Captain Fox," Fraser said as they parted. "We must hurry. My orders call for me to call at Marmorice Bay, where the fleet assembles, and failing that to proceed straight to Alexandria — or, rather, to Abukir Bay, where the landings will be made. The plans were drawn up some time ago, and the secret has been kept."

Fox did not say: "It's been kept from me! I would far rather be on my way with Nelson to the Baltic!"

He remembered Abukir Bay.

By God! He'd know damn well where he would not take *Alkon!* He'd been on the point of plunging into the fray of what was now erroneously called the Battle of the Nile when *Culloden* had stuck fast. He'd sat and watched and sworn all night. He'd steer *Alkon* well clear of the shoals! Bigod, yes!

So it was that Fox bent every effort to coaxing the best speed from his new command ...

Although he was forced to stay in his allotted position with the convoy, he took the measures best known to his cunning and devious mind to improve the sailing qualities of *Alkon.*

In addition he tried out, with the scepticism of an old sea salt and the enthusiasm of a man with an eager prying mind anxious to test all new inventions, the theories of Captain Cowan. Captain Malcolm Cowan, from the Orkneys, maintained that sails should be made up with their seams horizontal instead of vertical. He also sewed in reef points at the foot of the sail as well as the head, and by these means claimed that the sail could be set and handed far more rapidly. It was said that the courses and top-gallants could be reefed from the deck and the topsails would need only one man. Cowan had been appointed last year by the Admiralty to supervise the making of his new sails. With this as warrant, and the direction from Their Lordships that the invention should be tried in the most ample manner, Fox set about the job.

The sailmaker shook his grey head and said that it waren't go nohow sir, and wouldn't-a-done for Benbow and suchlike professional conservatism. But Fox persevered.

He had no guns on his gun deck. He had a pair of eighteen-pounder carronades on his forecastle and just twelve nine-pounders, long guns, on his quarterdeck. If he could save men from the task of reefing and put them to serving his guns, he would do so. It took a man more than a year to become halfway proficient aloft. Fox could knock a gun crew halfway proficient inside a quarter-dozen floggings.

As to finding that mythical perfection he sought always and knew always to be only a chimera; he wouldn't find that on this voyage with *Alkon.*

The days passed, the February passed, and the weather continued fine and the passage ate up the sea miles.

Fox kept a jaundiced eye on his charts. The track of the convoy grew each day, each day's run meticulously logged. There had to be a break soon, and the weather would turn nasty. If there was to be some action ahead, then Fox wanted to get there before it was over. No one was going to notice the captain of a flute bringing stores after a battle.

Fraser elected, very sensibly, to sail to the south of Crete. He could then turn through a full right angle and run up to Marmorice Bay, with Rhodes to larboard, and so come safely to anchor.

Mr. Bembridge had the watch and the midshipman who knocked and entered Fox's cabin looked more than a little put out. His young face flushed and his jaw set at a stubborn angle. Fox looked up from Major Mansfield's chess board where he found himself in a most tricky position, with Mansfield all set to fork his rook and queen with a damned knight.

"Yes, Mr. Girling?"

"Mr. Bembridge's compliments, sir, and will you step up on deck." Here Girling swallowed, and went on: "He don't like the look o' the horizon to eastward, sir."

"Thank you Mr. Girling. I shall come on deck directly."

Girling, very stiff, departed. Fox sighed. That idiot Bembridge was enough to get up any man's nose. Still, he knew now why Bembridge required his presence on the quarterdeck.

"Storms coming, captain?"

"We have been extraordinarily fortunate so far, major. If we are in for a blow we can blame no one."

"I have urgent business with General Abercromby. If the landings go forward before we arrive —"

"I have a feeling, major, they will not."

Mansfield looked his surprise.

Fox did not enlighten him but went up on deck.

Bembridge was right.

No sailorman would care to savour what that angry, brassy light portended. Thick clouds massed ahead. Fox stood, feeling the air, feeling the wind, feeling the surge and pitch of the ship. In any well-found vessel with courses, topsails and top-gallants set and with spanker and fore-topmast staysail and jib drawing, nothing much more than seven degrees of heel would be tolerated if you held her up to six points off the wind. Fox sniffed.

83

The wind was veering. The shift if it continued would not seriously impede the convoy until that turn was made to take them up northwards towards Marmorice Bay. Fox glanced at the signal midshipman and young Mr. Hardcastle jumped as though goosed and feverishly scanned the hoists breaking out from *Jubilee.*

Fox had no need to bellow a scathing: "Look alive there, Mr. Hardcastle."

Over six weeks of example had shown the crew of *Alkon,* officer and hand alike, just what Commander Fox wanted done and just how damned fast he wanted it done, into the bargain.

The black balls broke and Hardcastle babbled off the numbers.

"Reduce sail to conform," said Bembridge.

"Make it so," said Fox.

Reducing sail did not fit in with his plans at all.

The gale when it struck swirled up around them in clouds that pressed black and bellowing. *Alkon* shuddered. The men had the canvas under control and only one luckless wight slipped and sprained an ankle and wrist.

"Take that man's name!" said Fox, incensed. The idea of pity for the idiot as he lay groaning and holding ankle and wrist by turn as his mates hurried up occurred to Fox. He dismissed it. Oh, yes, he felt sorry that a seaman had been injured, for the fool should never have slipped. Now he'd be stuck below in his hammock, useless, a pair of hands and feet that could not be pressed into the service of the ship.

Alkon heeled as the gale struck, recovered, bore away.

Fox might very well have been through many and many a gale; he treated each one with the respect it deserved and took no chances. He discovered that *Alkon* was not altogether as good a sea boat as he could wish. He had coaxed extra speed out of her; but he had done nothing to improve her sea keeping qualities in a heavy blow. The only thing to be done was to hold on.

For the rest of the day and most of the night the elements attempted to sink Fox's flute; but endurance of man and ship held out and in the end won, so that as the morning dawned, fiery and furious, with promise of more northerlies to come, Fox could survey the dripping scene and reflect that the worst was, for the time being, over.

"No sight of the convoy!"

Well, that was to be expected. Convoys scattered during a gale as a matter of self-protection as much as a matter of being driven asunder. The thought of careering down in the teeth of the wind on to another vessel of the convoy filled any commander with the shudders:

Here came Mr. Rattray, the master, touching his hat in the new style, which sat ill on his elderly manners, saying: "The convoy'll be well to the nor'rard, sir."

Fox knew the master was correct.

"Maybe, maybe, Mr. Rattray," he said, making his voice at once firm and yet not hostile. "There is every chance they will have been driven further south than we have."

Rattray pursed his lips. Fox fancied he was not so much contemplating the possible awful consequences of arguing with a captain as debating the grounds of Fox's claim.

"We ran full and free, sir. I'm thinking Captain Fraser and the others will have hung up as hard as they could so as not to lose their northing —"

"We'll maintain our present course for the moment, Mr. Rattray. East a half north. If we run too far north we'll lose precious time. Time, Mr. Rattray, is of the essence."

"Absolutely correct, Captain," came Major Mansfield's drawl, and Fox turned to see the light cavalryman braced on the quarterdeck, muffled up, chin lifted, staring with calculating eyes at him.

Fox remembered that awkward knight fork of his rook and queen.

He knew, instinctively and without question, that Mansfield knew what he was going to do.

Rattray was clearly puzzled. To reach Marmorice Bay they must steer as closely north as they could, and might make too many boards for any captain's liking until they did. The master could very clearly see that to steer too far north too soon might mean cutting the wakes of the convoy. Fox, watching, saw the master mentally give up his protestations. He would settle for obeying his captain for, after all, Fox was not hazarding the ship.

They stood on the quarterdeck with the wind still blustering from the north-west and *Alkon* plunging on over the deep and long rollers that spoke eloquently of the past gale. Spume flew from her forefoot and Fox judged that he might take the reefs out of the topsails. At each stage of the process he felt the surge of his vessel beneath him, judging the moment when she was not doing all she could, and then feeling the shock of the resumed onward attack on the waves as the reefs shook out. Fox kept his command sailing right up to the limit of the canvas she would bear. As Nelson would say, lose not a moment.

He had not slept much in the last thirty-six hours. That was no novelty. The routine of the ship went on smoothly; he had a master-at-arms he felt he could trust. Mr. Baker was a hard and ruthless man, as he must be; but Fox had watched him at work and judged he was a fair specimen of that terrible breed, the master-at-arms. The Boatswain was just such another old salt as the master, as the purser, as the gunner. They probably had a little blood mixed in with the rum and seawater in their veins.

George Abercrombie Fox had to work ahead and to think most clear-headedly about his next orders. The sailing master would obey his orders to take his ship anywhere he chose if the ship was not hazarded. Rattray would not dare to question his orders on any other grounds. But the right words must be spoken so that, at any possible court-martial, they would produce the correct effect on his judges. Fox had done this before. He set to this time with a will.

"I fear we will never catch the convoy now, gentlemen," he said, at large.

Had Carker or Grey heard him talk like that they'd have known on the instant that he was up to devilry.

"With respect, sir," said Rattray, rabbitting away at being a good master. "I believe we are not too much to loo'ard o' them, sir. We can bear up a few points yet and rendezvous in Marmorice Bay." He looked a little prideful as he spoke, conscious of his own sailing and navigational abilities.

Devil take the old fogey and his pride in sailing!

"It is my judgement we would be late, Mr. Rattray. Captain Fraser was explicit upon the point. It is there in black and white in the orders." These orders Fox had asked for and obtained — he had not relished that sailing blind from England. "Our first duty is to carry the supplies to General Abercromby."

He could see Mansfield nodding his head. Was there a hint of a smile on those mobile lips? Damn the Canuck, anyway, if he thought to beguile G.A.F. Fox wasn't doing this to please a jingling light cavalryman seconded to some corps of guides or other; George Abercrombie was doing this so as to get himself into the thick of it, where he might pick up a little notice with subsequent letters in the *Gazette* — and a hatful of prize money if anything happened by. Bigod, yes!

He'd let Rattray give the orders to wear ship. They'd be running full and bye, and so with a little careful persuasion of *Alkon,* could expect to cover the distance in fine style.

"I shall be much obliged, Mr. Rattray, if you will make a course to take us direct to Egypt. Abukir Bay."

And George Abercrombie Fox stuck his hands up into the small of his back and stalked off to that sacred weather side of the quarterdeck well pleased with himself.

Chapter Eight

That white triangle danced ominously in the field of his glass.

The far-off gleam hung against the horizon rim, keeping its distance, hovering, waiting.

George Abercrombie Fox felt something of the tortures a man in Dante's Inferno must feel when the red-hot pincers drew off portions of his anatomy.

He'd made his decision, out of wilfulness, stubbornness, the selfish desire to do great things and make a stir and grab prize money — all for his family, true, but still all selfish motives against the wider implications of the war — and his act had brought disaster.

He should have borne up for the convoy. That damned Frog privateer or sloop or corvette over there would have thought twice about tangling with *Jubilee.* That the privateer would have made an attack of some kind remained certain; but any subsequent loss of British ships would have been fortunes of war. Now, if Fox was taken, he would have hazarded his ship. He should have stuck with the convoy.

That was what convoys were for.

He had no delusions about French fighting capacity at sea. It was fashionable to sneer at the Frogs as seamen; and it was true they never somehow seemed to get the hang of what naval battles were all about. The reasons for that, Fox suspected, having been in France and having seen things with his own evil eyes, was the overwhelming preponderance of the French Army. The army had brought glorious victories to La Belle France. This maniac Bonaparte was a damned fine soldier, for all he was a villainous scoundrel. The French people were heart and soul with their army; they didn't care about their navy. The French navy felt isolated, discarded, disregarded.

Exactly the reverse situation obtained in England.

Fox knew the whole country would thrill to a great feat of arms on the high seas. The country believed in the navy, its sure shield and defence. And — the Navy was hardly likely to land and march on the Houses of Parliament and hang the king and take over the country. Armies did that kind of thing.

That damned privateer was growing bolder — Fox could see her courses now, and even as he looked, steadying the glass with the instinctive grace of the born sailorman, her black streak of hull broke fitfully into view. She was coming down sniffing, for her yards had not braced around. She held the wind. Fox, ruminating about the way England regarded her army with contempt and ridicule, deliberately turned around in the main cross trees, wedging his back against the mast, and studied every point of the horizon.

They were alone on the blue sea.

There had been a continuous succession of northerly blows, the remnants of gales bellowing down over the Mediterranean from the conjoined winds from the Aegean and the southern shores of Turkey. There was absolutely no chance now whatsoever of clawing back.

Fox gave a last long look at their pursuer,

He fancied she'd be a privateer, rather than a National ship. She'd have one or two heavy long guns, a couple of batteries of eight pounders, and probably — if he was so unlucky — a few brass howitzers, fifty pounders, very likely.

She'd be fast. There was no question of her being anything else. She'd have anything from two to three hundred men in her. Her captain would be a good seaman, for France produced first class sailors. Her men would be of exactly the stamp of men Fox understood — out for plunder.

Bigod!

He wasn't going tamely to surrender his ship. He'd fight.

Having said that made him uneasy. When did any English sea officer have to promise himself he would fight Jack Corse? Dammit all to hell and gone! Just get the guns firing and the roundshot hurtling and set the game of bowls in action. Let all this high and mighty contemplation of national traits be whiffed away in the bellow of the guns and the choking swirl of gunpowder, let it all vanish will o' the wisp in the hard practical subjects of which he was a master.

Fox descended the shrouds with a quick and nimble grace, his chunky body perfectly adapted to the demands of shipboard life. The instant his shoes hit the deck he was bawling his orders. "Mr. Colledge, lay her on the larboard tack, if you please!"

"Hands to the braces! Headsail sheets! Cheerly there now, cheerly!"

He could guess what that French privateer skipper was thinking. He'd have seen *Alkon* fairly, observed the way she plugged along, the way she handled, the fashion in which her sails drew. He'd recognise her for a British man-of-war, and would therefore be cautious. He'd hold off, making sure that this vessel for whose cargo he hungered was really a warship and not some merchant ship dressed up to look ferocious. No doubt he'd have experience of Indiamen with painted gun ports. That Frog skipper might know of the fleet sailing with Lord Keith, and know there were Indiamen pressed into government service, might conceivably imagine this lone sail to be a straggler. Storeship, then, the Frenchman would be thinking. Perhaps his thoughts would go further and his agile mind would be contemplating the possibility — en flute?

Either way, Fox did not intend to give the Frog time to contemplate too long. As the pipes twittered and the hands boiled up on to the deck with that blood stirring sound of horny naked feet pattering on wooden planking, Mr. Colledge went about the evolution. There was good reason behind this employment at this juncture of Mr. Colledge. Fox, his face unreadable, knowing he put the fear of God in the hands, walked carefully to stand in his accustomed place not too far from the wheel and the binnacle, out of the way of the officer of the deck, watching with an implacable eye every evolution Mr. Colledge would perform.

Colledge was clearly sensible of the importance of the manoeuvre. Simple enough, a mere coming to the wind and a bracing up on to the larboard tack; but Fox had been giving a reasonable amount of time to the problem of Colledge — not too much, just the sufficient quantity he considered any competent captain should give to a thick-headed subordinate — and he fancied that simple though the evolution was, Colledge would treat his captain's thus placing the work into his hands as a kind of cachet. For all the sullenness had left Mr. Colledge the moment Fox had decided to bear away for Abukir Bay. The difference had been amazing. There was no real way Fox, as captain, could get to the bottom of the affair without making much too much fuss. But he suspected with his shrewd insight into men of this stamp that Colledge had been suffering from the same malady as afflicted Fox himself. Now, this direct run to Egypt might provide a successful antidote.

That could only be, of course, if this damned French privateer could be frightened or foxed off.

Alkon came to the wind, heeled a little too loosely for Fox's appreciation, began to beat her way into the northwards close-hauled. She did not handle well close-hauled.

Fox decided to let his men know what was afoot.

He lifted his head, disdaining a speaking trumpet, bawled viciously into the sweet Mediterranean air.

"What of the chase, you jackanapes whoreson?"

The lookout screeched down, startled.

"No change, sir! She's holding her wind."

Fox let rip a remark about holding his wind that brought vast grins across the faces of the hands within earshot, grins of outrageous insubordination that were wiped away instantly as Fox swung his ugly face at them.

Now, had it been Wilson up there, or Landsdowne, that information would not have had to be asked for. They'd know their captain would want to know everything before it happened.

Mr. Rattray, somewhat stiff about his walk, his hands at his sides, clearly intended to open a conversation. His old face looked more set in glue than ever.

"Well, Mr. Rattray?"

"Do you mean to fight, sir?" cried Rattray. "For, by God, sir, we'll have yonder scoundrel by the heels in a trice!"

"No doubt, Mr. Rattray, no doubt." About to comment acidly on a crew of old men and boys, Fox realised that Rattray did not consider himself an old man. You had to admire the old fogey. His silver hair and bulbous nose at this moment gave a feeling of vast confidence, most strange.

"We'll fight the bastard if we have to, Mr. Rattray. But my orders are to get into Abukir Bay as soon as humanly possible. On this occasion we may run without dishonour."

Major Mansfield, as ever there and inconspicuous when he wanted to be, nodded. He no doubt saw things with a soldier's eye; even an idiot could see *Alkon* was in no case to fight a ship crammed with men. Trouble was, most of the navy were far gone past the stage of being idiots when it came to counting the odds against them.

Fox bellowed at Mr. Midshipman Girling, loud enough so that the word would precede the flying form of the mid: "Mr. Shippey, Mr. Weston, Mr. Shaw to lay aft, Mr. Girling. Lively now, you imp of Satan."

"Aye aye, sir!" screeched young Girling, haring off, his blue coat and white trousers animated by a very pressing desire to do what this black bastard of a captain said at once.

The boatswain, the carpenter, the gunner, congregated with Fox aft by the taffrail. Old service men, grizzled warrant officers, they stood awaiting the orders they might be given, ever ready to question them in the way of the shell-backed service, and to carry them out with the faultless precision of long experience.

Fox stared around on them with that lowering, intolerant, devilish look transfiguring his face.

"Now, gentlemen," he said in his brusque, damn-you-to-hell voice. "If you do not wish to kick your heels in some stinking Frog prison you will attend to my orders with the utmost attention."

They listened.

The plan, as simple and direct as Fox could make it, had them scurrying about their business. The boatswain could be relied on, as could the carpenter. The gunner would need to be checked as to his display of technical proficiency, and Fox wasn't going to be fobbed off with anything less than the best the gunner could offer.

Alkon heeled to the breeze and the spume flew and Fox resolutely kept his eyes inboard.

"You'll have to rig eyebolts, for there's none here," he said, bearing down, making them see both the urgency and the awful responsibility at hand. The carpenter and the boatswain nodded, sucking their teeth, just two more old shell-backed warrant officers who found they could talk in their own arcane and technical language to a fancy quarterdeck officer and receive as good as they got — better, as they quickly found out.

Fox knew about British long nines.

Reputed the most accurately bored of all British sea ordnance, the long nine could be relied on to shoot straight. Fox knew well enough what he could do in the way of accurate shooting with any piece if he knew the beast. The exercises he had performed with *Alkon's* crew, over and over, on the voyage out had included only a modest apportionment of real firings. This commission had been undertaken quickly, quicker, even, than that custom of the service it so much resembled when a captain took up a post because the post captain of the ship was temporarily away — sick or attending Parliament, for example — and some poor devil on the beach on half-pay took up an acting command. So Fox had been unable to grease the palm of some unctuous Ordnance or dockyard official who could supply him with extra powder.

Fox's memory harked back to Acre and the way he'd cap-a-barred a battery of Boney's artillery. He'd blown the caissons up with a single shot. That was the way the story went. In actuality there had been two shots; but both the guns had been laid by him and they'd fired at the same time.

With the work aft on the quarterdeck going on well and with the prospect of having a nine pounder spiked around and

95

breeched in good time, Fox saw that his play would have to be used.

Alkon bore on, sturdily if resentful of lying over like this with her canvas stiff as boards, heeling and plunging, sheeting sleeting spume across her forecastle. The Frenchman grew in size rapidly. He was coming down. The ruse of frightening him off had not worked.

En flute ...

No. Not with twelve nine pounders and a couple of carronades. And a crew of cripples and children.

So he was exaggerating. Fox never could stand running from a fight; but this was one fight in which he knew he'd be in for a licking to nothing. No one could censure him for running. It was his duty to bring these stores in so the army could fight — that army that was so ridiculed — and not to become embroiled in a useless fight against a saucy French privateer.

"Put the ship about, if you please Mr. Colledge."

Colledge gave the necessary orders, again, as Fox could see, pleased to be entrusted with the task. The officer of the deck might glower; Fox could have done the job himself, or given it to the master. As it was, he sowed his bread upon the waters. *Alkon* swung about, her canvas handled with a dexterity that pleased Fox and the old ship straightened up on her new course.

Fox looked aloft

Now he was running. He felt the heave of the deck beneath his feet. He felt the wind. More canvas was essential; the way of it would matter. Very often a ship's best point of sailing was with the wind on her quarter. Fox was always partial to a vessel whose best point of sailing was close-hauled. It seemed to him, feeling the ship, thinking about her lines, visualising the calculations, knowing what he had learned of *Alkon,* that she would sail best with the wind further around astern than purely on the quarter. No captain liked running with the wind directly astern; broachings to and awful accidents of like horror might befall. But old *Alkon* could certainly lift her skirts with the breeze blowing fairly up them.

Fox gave the course, south east, and then said: "I'll be obliged, Mr. Colledge, if you'd set the royals;"

Mr. Rattray gave a nervous start.

"Aye aye, sir," said Colledge, spritely as a cricket. All his sullenness had dropped from him.

Mr. Rattray cast a profoundly gloomy glance aloft, and softly he tut-tutted to himself.

To cheer up the old fogey, Fox said: "I fancy we'll set the stun's'ls soon, Mr. Rattray."

"She'll not like it, sir." Rattray shook his head. "She'll not care for it at all, sir."

Rattray evidently was at home with the captains who would never set their royals from hoisting the commissioning pendant to dropping the hook ready to be paid off.

"She'll ride it, Mr. Rattray. She's a rare plucked 'un, is *Alkon.*"

"Oh, aye, sir. Not a doubt of it." Here Rattray twisted his neckcloth as though it had miraculously changed into a serpent of the Nile itself. "The fore royal mast isn't all I'd like, sir, in the matter of soundness."

Fox knew this. Hadn't he bashed the bloody thing and heard the dull note in place of the solid ring?

"She'll take it, Mr. Rattray. See how she flies along!"

Everyone appeared delighted with *Alkon's* performance. The lookout sang out: "Deck there! She's gaining!"

That could dampen enthusiasm. Even with *Alkon* giving her utmost the Frenchman still gained. Fox leaped up on to the lower ratlines and gazed back. His gaze fastened evilly upon their pursuer. Yes! The bastard was sailing three feet to their two. Plan one had failed, and therefore plan two must be pressed into business.

As though fully conscious of the captain's thoughts, the boatswain and the carpenter came forward.

"All squared away?" demanded Fox, leaping from the shrouds and starting aft. He could see the nine-pounder, spiked around, fresh tackles rigged, the breechings hugging her like a mother hugs her baby. Her crew stood ready, ramrod, sponge, worm. A cheese of wads, a selection of infernal rigging-cutting shot, a priming powder horn. Fox looked at the brown faces of the men, observing.

"Right," he said, and, most theatrically, rubbed his hands together. "Now let's see if we can knock that poxed Frog's nose off for him."

The hands enjoyed this sort of rough knockabout humour. They knew a fight was imminent, and, moreover, a fight in which they stood every chance of taking a good licking. But whilst the captain was prepared to act as he was, their spirits remained high. Goddamn 'em! thought Fox. They'd remain with spirits high when the Frogs poured over in a flood of raving assassins. One most significant item would not have been overlooked by the hands. Fox had given no orders to clear for action ...

He selected a nine pounder round shot from those presented. He held it in his hands, feeling around it with his palms, as he had felt Jennie's breast in Tunbridge Wells, or delicious Kitty Higgins' in *Tiger,* or a countless host of other girls, come to that. He felt the heavy roundness of the ball.

He nodded, satisfied that the shot, true or not, would suffice. There would be time. The last time he'd done this the range had been coming down all the time, so fast it had been all nip and tuck. Whilst the crew loaded, for the gun had been drawn so as to obviate the foolishness of shooting with damp powder, Fox stared aft. The privateer looked beautiful. Well, any full-rigged ship, under all plain sail and with studding sails set, booming along, proud and alive and glorious, looked beautiful. The bone in her teeth was not overlarge. She was slipping through the water. *Alkon* was bludgeoning her way through.

As he looked a puff of white broke from the forecastle.

The shot whistled past, making an infernal whining din, plunged into the sea ahead of them. A twenty-four, probably.

"Right, lads," said Fox, again acting his part. "We'll have the bastard in a moment or two."

He took deliberate aim, bending to peer along the line of metal, disdaining the dispart sight. He wanted to know how his body and brain, all his senses, reacted to the accuracy of this one particular gun. Arching over, he pulled the lock string and the gun bellowed and belched and barrelled back on its trucks under his body.

Everyone watched for the fall of shot.

Close, into the water half a cable's length short, and a trifle to larboard.

The brownish yellow smoke blew stingingly back from the gun, dissipating in the breeze. Now Fox could point to the elongating shot he fancied. This was always a tricky business, particularly for this special brand for the nine pounder. But he knew what he knew about guns, and trajectories, and the arcane lore of fired gunpowder and the way mulishly obstinate chunks of iron flew their own mysterious courses through the air.

This time as he peered along the line of metal with his right eye he knew that his left eye had not closed up, and he didn't give a damn if it did. But his refractory left eye remained perfectly capable as an orb of vision, as the surgeons put it. He quoined the gun down by a fraction — that artful, professional, knowing fraction, and said: "Spike her around to starboard — a little more — handsomely — steady — belay!"

Now was the moment for play acting.

"For what those bastard Frogs are about to receive," he said, full voiced, happy, confident, "May they be truly repentant." He jerked the lock string.

The nine pounder flamed and roared and the smoke blew and the sniff of it was like wine to a war charger, and everyone yelled and threw their hats off and stamped and bellowed.

Over there the privateer's foretop-gallant mast had bent and bowed, like some fop of the ancien régime, bent lower and snapped and gone plunging down into the bowsprit. There was one hell of a mess in that ship. The driver sent her surging around, she flew up into the wind, and the bowsprit, the last Fox saw of it, looked as though it had wrenched itself off at the gammoning. Capital! Oversparred like the best French vessels, the privateer had snapped her poxy nose right off her face.

"One shot!"

Fox heard the excited calls and shouts, spreading the word throughout the ship. He let the pandemonium last for perhaps three heartbeats. He needed those to get his wind. Then:

"Belay that jabbering, you pile of heaping blagskites! You're like a pack o' Rock monkeys! Stow your gabs! Mr. Colledge! Hand the stun's'ls and the fore-royal! Cheerly, now, you lollygagging pile of layabouts! And silence! If there's any more monkey chattering I'll have a score o' red checked shirts at the gangways!"

They knew enough about their captain, this maniac, this black bastard Fox, to know he meant what he said.

The hands rushed aloft to clear the straining masts of their freight of canvas. Fox looked back. The Frog was dropping away fast; long before he had the raffle cleared and was under way again night would have fallen and *Alkon* had a clear run.

"Capital, sir, capital!" Mr. Rattray was bubbling over.

Fox took no great pride. That had not been a lucky shot. Oh, of course, any shot that did that work was lucky; but the shot itself was the result of years of experience and an eye.

"My congratulations, Captain Fox." Major John Mansfield knew about artillery. "A remarkable shot, sir."

"No," said George Abercrombie Fox. "No, major. Not remarkable. Just necessary."

Chapter Nine

"My oath!" said Major John Mansfield. "What a sight!"

The whole southern horizon grew the masts of ships.

"A most pleasing sight to contemplate," observed Mr. Rattray, with the self-satisfied complacency of a sailing master casting a critical eye over the ships of his peers.

Alkon bore on, the sea still running a swell after the continual series of northerlies; but the Bay would soon be calm enough to disembark the troops, and Fox had his own brand of ideas on that.

There had been no need to hoist the private signal when they'd borne up for the French privateer, for the situation then had been clear cut. Now *Alkon* made her number, and with a promptitude entirely pleasing to the critical faculties of a sea officer, the flagship hoisted Fox's instructions to report. What was not so pleasing was the sober contemplation of the way the coming interview with Lord Keith would go. The men bent to their oars and the boat flew across the water. These ships had been anchored up here for a few days, at the least, reflected

Fox. They'd anchored and then the swell had made it impossible to transfer the troops ashore — yes, that was the way of it. He'd only just made it, then, only just arrived up in the nick of time.

He went up the side of *Foudroyant* — for poor *Queen Charlotte* had burned, bad cess to the criminally insane idiots who had let that obscenity happen — and so, with first a midshipman and then a lieutenant and finally the flag lieutenant to lead the way down into the admiral's quarters.

Keith looked plump and well fed, very white about the hair, artfully waved and tangled in the fashion, and his eyes looked deeply set beside the large nose. Fox didn't much care for that resigned droop of the mouth. Keith had had a lot to put up with in his command in the Mediterranean. Nelson had been a prickly handful. Keith must have heaved a tremendous sigh of relief when Nelson went home. Still and all, in the strict admiralty pattern of naval life, Keith had been in the right of it, over that affair of sending ships to Minorca, for instance ... But Nelson was Nelson, and he had got handsomely away with it, his defence of Naples perfectly adequate to condone direct disobedience.

The interview was short. Keith had much to do. The landing in Abukir Bay had been held up by the weather, the ships riding here for five days so far and everything arranged for this very night as ever was, the 7th March, 1801. The great aft cabin glowed with light. The furnishings were simply gorgeous. *Foudroyant* had come out from England as a new ship and Nelson had taken her as his flagship. Fox thought of *Alkon,* and then braced up as the introductions were made.

"Major Mansfield! I am indeed glad to welcome you aboard, sir. You know poor Mackarras is killed? Major Fletcher and Major Mackarras were taken as they attempted to reconnoitre the beach — a sad business, sad, indeed."

"I am most pained to hear it, my lord," said Mansfield.

Fox didn't know either of the two majors of engineers stupid enough to be captured; but he saw that Mansfield was affected by the news. Fox kept very quiet, there in that gorgeous cabin, and waited until Mansfield's business was finished. He would play a more important part after the initial landing had been affected and the army was on the way to Alexandria.

The air of leave-taking was clear, now. The flag-captain shuffled papers, and the flag-lieutenant braced up, just as Fox had done, ready to conduct them out.

Fox stepped forward. He swallowed. He said: "By your leave, my lord. I have taken great pains to arrive here in time — I am known to Sir Sidney Smith and would greatly value your lordship's permission to be appointed to boat service tonight."

Tonight was the seventh, the sea had only just moderated enough for the flat-bottom boats carried aboard the merchantmen to be trusted to swim, and the crews were going mad hoisting the boats out and chivvying the soldiers down into them. Fox scented battle.

Admiral Lord Keith looked at him with that kind of look that clearly said: "Queenie would have nothing to do with you, young man, in a single one of her routs."

Not that Fox was ever likely to be invited to Lady Keith's. He was not of that charmed circle. And that meant that by that amount he was less likely to be offered anything useful. He just stood there, lumpy, the uniform that had appeared so dashing and fine in Portsmouth now revealed as a shabby, cheap, lack-lustre abomination, and the nakedness of his right shoulder stood as an affront in that glittering state cabin.

"Sir Sidney?"

"I had the honour to serve under him at Acre, my lord."

"Really? But you must know how boat service is requested by all the young bloods — I really do not know."

"With permission, my lord, may I speak with Sir Sidney?"

"Speak with him?" Keith hummed and hawed. He'd give nothing away. Only one thing stood in Fox's favour; he was not known as a faction man, and it was sure that Keith would not have heard of Fox's mad dash to Yarmouth — thank God!

"Yes, Captain Fox, by all means — speak to Sir Sidney."

"My warmest thanks, my lord."

So George Abercrombie withdrew before he spewed all over that fancy deck with the black and yellow chequers, over the gorgeous spectacle of a peer of the realm in all his pride and glory.

The last thing Keith said — so typical, the last — was:

"Are you related to General Abercromby, captain?"

"I do not have that honour, my lord."

Mansfield came up on to the deck with him and walked along the gangway. They shook hands.

"I shall be with the general, I assume, captain. But I would esteem it a great pleasure if you could find time to visit."

"If we get ashore," said Fox, darkly, "I shall avail myself of your kind invitation with much pleasure."

He went down into the boat, wondering if he'd ever see Major John Mansfield again.

Tigre was much as he remembered. The weird repetition of going aboard, amid all the hurly burly of the seamen preparing for their part in the night's operations, made him suck in his cheeks. He felt very much the interloper, very much the johnny-come-lately in this urgent bustle.

Sir Sidney Smith was ferociously busy.

"Captain Fox? Acre?" He looked up, his thin face quizzical. "Yes, I remember. I am happy to renew our acquaintance, Captain Fox."

Fox put it to him, straight.

Smith frowned. "Every officer wishes to go, Captain Fox. You must realise that."

"I do indeed, sir. But I am able to furnish a boat and crew, willing to go on any service —"

With the decision that any naval officer should cultivate, Smith made up his mind. Men laughed at him, called him the Knight of the Sword — and now, since he would go on so about the famous siege of Acre, they called him Long Acre — but men also recognised his restless genius. "You may take your boat — you have a two-pounder? Good — and support the left flank of the assault." It was not at all strange to hear this man talking about flanks, where it would come deucedly odd in most other naval officers.

Fox let his breath out.

"Thank you, sir. I am most deeply indebted —"

"If your head is blown off, captain, how much will you thank me, then?"

Fox chanced his arm.

"It wasn't blown off in the breach at Acre — sir."

Smith's quick, energetic manner took something of the effect of a backed maintopsail at this. He looked at Fox with that shrewd sharpness of his. "Let me tell you this, sir. I am ordered to liaise with the Turkish fleet under the Captain Pasha. Major General Sir John Moore has made an inspection of the Grand Vizier's army, from which was hoped so much, even after they've been beat silly by the rascally French." Here Smith let his sharp eyes dart a most meaningful glance at Fox. "You'll not find the Turks the same men as those with whom we fought at Acre, sir!"

This was a clear opening. Fox wanted to know all he could, and opportunities like this came seldom. "I am given to understand, sir, we have an army under General Baird advancing from Bombay up the Red Sea — take the Frogs from the south —"

"I'll believe in 'em when I see 'em," snapped Smith.

Fox kept his bronzed old figurehead entirely impassive. Much as he loved dabbling in the waters of the higher command he knew when to haul up. He'd proved to himself that he was capable of high command in the navy. Admiral Cloughton could testify to that — it seemed to Fox that Smith must have heard of the action in which Cloughton's force of four of the line had succeeded in blowing up two, taking two and making the remaining three, outwitted, run. If so he made no reference to it, although, busy as he was and making ready to go down into the launch, he more than once referred to Acre ...

"Captain Cochrane of *Ajax* is commanding the boats, captain. I am detailed to take charge of the field artillery and the landing party of hands."

Seizing on the minutest gap in the flow of words so as to appear he was not interrupting, Fox cracked out: "With your permission, sir, I would esteem it an honour to serve with the landing party rather than with the boats." Again, thinking he knew his man and what greasy flattery might do, he added: "I have had experience of your leadership, sir, and greatly though I admire Captain Cochrane, feel I would best serve my country under your command."

It was gross. It was sickening. But for what Fox had in mind it was vitally necessary.

To be stuck out in the Bay in a flute, issuing supplies, whilst battles and actions went forward ashore, and his itchy fingers were unable to get at the purses of French soldiers, loaded with the plunder of the East! It was intolerable — it was unthinkable.

Smith, a vain man at the best of times, took the bait, and the hook bit.

"You are very kind in your sentiments, Captain Fox. I can make arrangements —" And, looking at him, Fox realised — and with a sudden and genuine shock — that Smith had calculated that this hard-faced, horny-handed tarpaulin sea officer would be a most useful subordinate.

So it was settled. Fox had argued closely and flatteringly, and had won what he desired.

No wonder he felt like letting rip a wild screeching Indian war cry of the kind he had heard the Redskins yell as they whooped into the attack, thirsting for scalps.

"The boats rendezvous on *Mondovi,* under Captain Stewart. She is anchored a gunshot from the beach. The dressing will be from the right. You will join me as soon as possible."

"Thank you, sir, your servant sir," and Fox took himself off.

He badly needed a drink — a drink of anything — to wash the taste from his mouth. But a flashing inward glimpse of his mother and his family, down there in the little house by the Thames, and the squalling brats with ever open mouths, convinced him, where no further convincing was necessary, that his determination to do anything at all for their welfare was the only course he could follow and remain at anything like peace with himself.

Back in *Alkon* he roused Mr. Colledge and sent that worthy roaring into action. The marines were sent off to join the battalion for the landing commanded by Lieutenant-Colonel Walter Smith. Fox ran his mental eye down his watch list. He wished — bigod, how he wished! — he had his own old Raccoons, or Minions, or Nuthatches, here now. But their names would change with their ships in which they served. They were miles away, serving on the Brest blockade, or running convoys, or doing any one of the thousands of tasks the navy undertook in this war.

A few words to pierce the inner armour of Colledge might not come amiss.

"We assumed, Mr. Colledge, that we were stuck in a flute and destined to rot. I had thought, as I am sure you are aware, that we were ordered to the Baltic with Lord Nelson. Well, now we have a chance to make all this worthwhile. We have joined an armada of upwards of seventy ships and an army of 15,000 or more men."

The first lieutenant was a changed man.

"Indeed, yes, sir!" he cried. "And if the army won't stick to their work, then the navy will, by God!"

"I am aware," said Fox, speaking not so much in the blabbermouth Foxey way that so infuriated him when he was dealing with Grey or Carker; but rather in a reflective tone of voice that impressed even himself. "There have been some shameful episodes — Ferrol, Cadiz, North Holland, Helder, Genoa — but this time, Mr. Colledge, I have a feeling the army is going to surprise the navy."

"Amen to that, sir."

But, for all his words, Fox was as well aware as everyone else in the gathered fleet that this Sir Ralph Abercromby was a most singularly unlucky general. Nothing he had ever done had gone aright for him, or so it seemed. Last year there had been 10,000, sometimes 20,000, British soldiers swanning about in the Mediterranean with no idea of where to go or what to do. This descent upon Egypt, for all its high hopes, smacked very much of a forlorn hope, of a mere sop to get the redcoats to do *something.*

Thinking of soldiers, he said: "Have Major Mansfield's dunnage sent across to the flagship, if you please, Mr. Colledge."

"Aye aye, sir. 'Tis a pity the major's not making the landing with us Alkons, sir."

Fox marvelled. Somehow he fancied Sir Ralph would not allow Mansfield to land in the first wave. That would upset the Canadian. But, Mansfield was a cunning devil. He'd been about to deprive Fox of a rook that was the sole prop to the left hand side of the board, and Fox had castled to that corner, and Mansfield, expansively, had leaned back and said:

"I am exceedingly fond of Reynolds! How I dote on Reynolds!"

Fox, not looking up, about to move a pawn that would drop him into the excreta, paused.

"Reynolds?"

"Indeed, my dear Captain Fox. Every time I am in England I take every opportunity to see all I can of Reynolds."

"Indeed?" That pawn left the rook somewhat naked ...

"The flesh tints, the complexions, the — what? — the sensuousness I believe has been called the juicy opulence — your knight is a trifle exposed, I fancy — and the colour and textures give me constant delight."

"The knight will do very well where he is, major. As for your Sir Joshua, I have seen his work at the Society of Artists, and elsewhere — very fine, very fine, but —"

"But what, captain! Surely you would not elevate Ramsay or Gainsborough or Romney —"

"I shall elevate this bishop, and see what you make of that, major." Fox did not chuckle; but he felt amused at John Mansfield's transparent honesty, his attempt in adoration of Reynolds to throw Fox off the trick of it. Hazel eyes always had been attractive ... Sensuous flesh tints, the voluptuous buxomness of a Rubens lady. Well, Fox fancied, as he made sure Mr. Colledge missed not a single item in the proper preparation for the night's work, well, Mansfield and Reynolds were a likely combination and he wished them well of it. Tonight, with the sea gone down to a flat calm, and the stars massed above, twinkling and glittering away, would take men into very different circumstances from standing, eyeglasses lifted, in the charming and elegant surroundings of artists and models ...

The problem was not finding men willing to come; the devil of it was in telling those either too young or too old that he could not take them. Mr. Colledge was perfectly under the impression he would be going along. Had Fox been a post captain and not charged with any of the boat work, he would not have been able to leave his ship. Had he been a lieutenant he might have wheedled his way ashore. As a commander he hung in a limbo, able to go and able, also, to tell Mr. Colledge that the first lieutenant must stay by the ship.

Colledge was aghast, crestfallen, annoyed and — chagrined?

Yes, and Fox knew why. There would be no chance of catching the eye of the admiral stuck away in a storeship.

And, here, George Abercrombie knew he made a decision that, perhaps, was not his to make. Colledge, now he was over the sulks, had proved to be a fine tarpaulin lieutenant. In Fox's judgement the man did not possess those qualities necessary for command. However overweening and puffed with pride this may have been, as, indeed, it was, it eased Fox's mind as to the suitability of his action. He couldn't even feel very sorry for Colledge. The man had been made, he must know in his heart of hearts he would never be posted unless a miracle occurred — and here, Fox's faultless logic faltered. Should Colledge be the first lieutenant to some post captain in a dashing and victorious exploit, such as taking an enemy frigate in a sanguinary single ship encounter, he might be promoted in compliment to his captain in the way of the service. The chance seemed remote, judging by Colledge's attributes. No. There was nothing else for it. Fox had manoeuvred himself into a boat command, and he'd damn well do it, knowing that he would do the job better than Colledge and Colledge would be better employed in *Alkon.*

The very fact that Fox bothered his head over this detail gave a true indication that, although he had not lost his old Foxey ways, his mind was more taken with the trivia of command than heretofore.

The water was glass smooth. The boats were aswim at two o'clock on the morning of the eighth, and two bells later they were ready assembled in their neat lines, aligned on *Mondovi,* ready to begin the assault. Just over 5,000 soldiers were crammed into the boats, sitting with their muskets between their knees. The jacks rowed with the phlegmatic irony they exhibited towards lobsters, for had they not shipped soldiers on and off before, and all for nothing?

In perfect silence the armada of three hundred and twenty boats waited. At eight bells the signal cracked out. Instantly every oar struck the water. Feeling the momentousness of the occasion, Fox said: "Give way!"

The invasion of Egypt had begun,

Chapter Ten

George Abercrombie Fox intended to obey his orders with the punctiliousness to be expected of a sea officer. Then, after that, to hell with the orders. He was going hunting the shifting of his swab.

Any guilt he might feel was all washed away as the glittering morning light revealed the sandy shore of Abukir Bay, and the line of sandhills beyond. Dark clumps of colour crested those dunes, and the flash and twinkle of hundreds of musket barrels and sabres set up a glitter to match the sea. Thank God the water was like a millpond! The boats pulled in perfect order, impeccable lines, dressed from the right.

The first line consisted of the flat-bottomed boats, each carrying fifty men. The second line was formed from the ship's cutters, and the third was of launches towing astern.

Out on the left flank Fox could look westwards and see the whole spectacle, the impeccable dressing of the lines, see the way the boats swept forward. Bigod! This was a day!

Gun boats and a cutter kept each flank. Fox had to restrain his eager enthusiasm to bellow at his men to pull like the devil and so get into the shore fast. He must remain exactly on station, pacing the line, ready to perform the very necessary function which Sir Sidney had allotted him before he could land and join the seamen ashore.

To the rear the majestic forest of masts showed where the fleet awaited the outcome of the landing; ahead around the curving bay the French waited on a front of a mile and a half. They knew the English were coming. They had known for some time and they had gathered their forces. Fox had no idea how many men would oppose the landing; rumour had it that there were not above 15,000 French soldiers left in Egypt. If that jackass Menou concentrated northwards from Cairo he could meet the English on the beach and hurl them, broken and bloody, back into the sea.

With the sudden rap of a single shot and then the rataplan of a fusillade, the French guns opened up. Smoke puffed from the dunes. White water spouts rose like ghosts, twisting from the sea, rising in columns and then breaking and falling. The noise began to build into that devilish roaring tattoo of battle.

"The bastards!" exclaimed Mr. Midshipman Hardcastle, gripping his sword. "They're shooting at us!"

Fox favoured him with a look.

"A highly commendable observation, Mr. Hardcastle. Would you kindly moderate your language? Do not forget I am responsible for you young gentlemen's moral welfare. Bigod! I'll have the bosun take his cane to your bottom!"

"Aye aye, sir!" said Hardcastle and a smashing avalanche of water cascaded over them all.

"Hands to the balers!" bellowed Fox, blinking his eyes, taking off his hat and bashing the water from it. "Handsomely now! Or you'll swim the rest of the way in!"

The water went sleeting out of the boat. Fox stared along the line of boats. Yes, bigod! There — a cutter drifting back from the line, shattered, her oars all askew, broken and sinking. Men were tumbling out of her like Dorset ninepins.

"Make for that cutter!" bellowed Fox and Hardcastle thrust the tiller over. Young men on this trip, young men, putting their young bodies in the way of roundshot and grape. Colledge might not have fancied this too highly ...

Fox's boat cut across the rear of the lines and in a trice the hands were heaving sailors inboard, grabbing soldiers by their white cross belts, not caring if the fancy shakos went floating away.

"In you come, lobster!" roared Horny Pete, dragging a soldier bodily over the gunwale. He bashed him on the back so that he flew into the bottom boards and bent for another.

The soldiers were being dragged inboard like fish out of a mill pool.

Fox looked again at the line of boats. A big flat-bottomed boat had been hit fairly amidships and there were red coats everywhere in the water, white faces yelling, arms uplifted.

Another rescue boat shot off and Fox bellowed: "Hurry it up, you lollygagging blagskites! All inboard! Give way! Pull, you poxy-faced set o' blackguards! Pull!"

His boat could not take all the survivors; but he would take all he could until the gunwales shipped water, and then make for the beach. Blood stained the water. Men were shrieking. These were Guards, fine tough, upstanding men, men penned too long in ships and hungry for action. They came inboard in a fine flurry of scarlet coats and Fox eyed the gunwale and calculated and bellowed ferociously at the men to sit still and keep out of the way of the hands.

At his furious orders lines were flung overboard.

"Tail on to the lines, you lobsters!" bellowed Fox. "Swim for it and we'll tow you!"

An officer with a face more scarlet than his coat, and with bulging blue eyes, tried to clamber up over the transom.

Fox leaned over, his face as ugly as a constipated devil.

"Belay that, captain! Hang on to the line! Bigod! If you try to climb inboard I'll bash your skull in!"

The captain gobbled insane words, scrabbling at the transom.

Fox could make out: "You've taken the scum in! I'm an officer — the honourable —"

Fox didn't bother to hear the rest. He prised the gripping fingers free and gave the man a push.

"There's a rope, honourable captain! Hang on for your life!"

He swung back. The boat was dangerously low. The hands looked at him, their arms extended, the oar looms all parallel.

"Give way. Handsomely, now, or you'll have us all shipping water into our bellies."

The boat crept across the sea, shining and smooth, and around them dropped the pattering hail of hundreds of musket balls. The gunfire created a tremendous racket; Fox concentrated on conning his boat safely into the beach.

The plan called for the cutters to slide into the fifty foot gaps between the flat-bottomed boats so that all the soldiers would hit the beach as one. The launches carried artillery, as well as men, and the companies were arranged in depth instead of width, so that men of the same company would land in support of each other.

In the stern of each boat a grapnel or small boat anchor was carried ready to be slung overboard the instant the boat grounded. Then, when empty, the boat could be hauled off and out of the way.

"Get ashore, that is the first priority!" That was the order. There was to be no thought of orderly filling in by the flank, of closing up. Just as they landed so they were to form front and charge hell for leather for the Frogs.

Well, Fox grumped, watching the sandy shore and the glint of sunlight and the billowing clouds of smoke, hearing the explosions and the spitting patter of musketry about his ears, the French had dealt with British landings before. This time they'd be cocky and confident, veteran troops who had never been beaten, men who had seen off armies four and five times their number — and from what he heard Turkish armies ten times their number. He wouldn't soon forget that long wait in Acre for the Turkish army to relieve them, and the shattering disappointment when the French whiffed away that host in the smashing power of their squares, the headlong panache of their cavalry.

The beach was coming nearer ...

A guardsman abruptly leaped to his feet, clawing at his throat. A musket ball had pierced him through. As he collapsed Fox was bellowing and the body was pitched over-side. Water slopped inboard. Almost immediately another lobster yelled and tried to pull a shattered arm out of the way of a jack lustily hauling his oar.

Only a few more yards — already the men were ashore along to the right, scarlet lines running swiftly forward across the sand. Smoke blew, obscuring many of the details, but Fox fancied the right was well ashore. That flank was commanded by Sir John Moore, a general of whom everyone spoke highly, and he had the 23rd and the 28th together with the flank companies of the 40th. Blobs and lines of scarlet appeared and disappeared through the smoke. They were going great guns over on the right. Around to the centre the 42nd and the 58th under Brigadier Oakes also seemed to be getting ashore. What the hell was going on straight ahead, on the left flank?

117

The boats were not moving forward. Masses of men were milling there, out of the boats, wading in the sea.

Bigod! The boats had grounded in shallows, some way from the beach!

Even as this fact registered Fox's boat hit. It lurched, groaned as the timbers ploughed through wet sand, came to a dead stop.

"All out!" Fox screamed. "Get ashore! Get ashore!"

A soldier leaped overboard and fell and did not rise. Blood drifted away from his body in the water.

The others were leaping over now, splashing through the shallows. The troops had been ordered to land with muskets unloaded, a very sensible precaution. They'd not be able to load until they reached the dry sand.

A mass of water abruptly upreared from the sea, golden with sand, curving, belching down on to the men in the water:

"Get on! Get on!" roared Fox, waving his arms.

The honourable captain appeared, drawing himself up with water pouring from him, his gorgeous uniform a sodden wreck.

"I'll have you —" he began.

"Get yourself ashore, captain, and take command of those men! For God's sake, you pimping whoreson! Move yourself! *Look!*"

The captain followed Fox's pointing finger. His eyes went wide. He gulped.

Down across the beach, galloping into the shallows and spouting great sheets of shining water charged the French cavalry!

"What are you?" yelled Fox. "Guardsmen! Well, get in there, lobster!"

Fox knew well enough the British were raw. They'd had no succession of unbroken victories to give them the supreme confidence of the fighting man in his own prowess. And now, here they were, pitchforked on to a foreign beach, wading ashore, and all unformed, being charged by those legendary French cavalry. Bigod! It was enough to make a man un-constipated for life.

The 2nd and 3rd Guards and the 54th must meet this challenge now. They must find their soul, find what had given their forefathers the victory at Blenheim and Malplaquet and Ramillies, at Crécy and Agincourt. If the left flank went the French would roll up the landing, piece by piece, tumble the whole British force back in bloody gobbets into the sea.

The noise spouted skywards. Men were struggling in the wet and slipping sand to wade ashore. Some already there were desperately trying to form.

Fox threw himself the length of the boat. He'd taken Mr. Shaw, the gunner, for the man ought to have expertise enough to keep a two-pounder dry. The gun was loaded and rammed. The cavalry were too close now to the blobs of scarlet across the beach. The soldiers would have to face this first smashing charge of cavalry alone and unaided. But the second wave, galloping hard on the heels of the first, plumes flying, pennons waving, their sabres all aligned, diabolically beautiful and evil — yes, that little lot could do with the medicine delivered by the Royal Navy.

The French were dragoons, roaring on, sabres glittering, hooves glittering, harness glittering, eyes and teeth glittering — Fox bent to the touchhole and the two-pounder, stuffed to the muzzle with grape, banged away with a jovial jack tar roar. Acrid smoke choked and bit and Fox, bellowing at Shaw and the gun crew, stared hungrily up the beach.

The grape scythed into the dragoons.

This discharge swept them away, men and horses rearing and falling, screaming, colliding in a sliding confused mass of disaster. Devilish, horrible — those poor damned horses — but necessary if five thousand British soldiers were not to be rolled up and flung back to drown.

"Bigod!" said Fox. "Damnation take 'em!"

Following the cavalry, running with skirmishers out, with their ragged clumping column that had conquered Europe, came the French infantry. A demi-brigade who advanced as they had done on a hundred battlefields and never known defeat —

Wait!

These must be the very men Fox had seen reeling back, confused, unbelieving and broken, from the beach at Acre!

If no one in Europe had been able to beat the French soldiers then they'd certainly been beat — aye, and with the maniacal Corsican Bandit at their head — at Acre by a few Turkish irregulars and by the Royal Navy. Fox knew. He'd been there.

The gun was loaded. He bashed out his orders and men had to leap into the shallows to shift the boat around bodily. Lightened by her landed burden of humanity, she was not difficult to move.

"Belay!" The gun muzzle leered upon the advancing infantry. This kind of warfare demanded different terms of calculation. The range was right — and there would be an opportunity for a second shot — Fox touched her off and instantly was roaring the crew to reload.

The head of the advancing infantry veered away.

The others came on at a rush, slipping and sliding over the sand. Poor devils, this was desperate work ...

Another gunboat opened up. The infantry came on.

The guards and the 54th, all mixed up, a blazing swirl of scarlet, were bashing at the cavalry, musket and bayonet against sabre. The shrieking and yelling, the neighing of horses, the distant clatter of metal, spilled down the beach with the uproar of a Bedlam. Fox eyed the cavalry.

They were not getting the best of it, bigod!

The British infantry, unformed, and untried, had taken that charge and were busily occupied in a confused and hand-to-hand struggle, dragging men from their saddles, cutting 'em up, showing the French veterans what fighting British soldiers was going to mean in the years ahead.

That was a mortal desperate affray going on up there ...

The gun was ready. Some of the infantry had broken off their jumbling spirited onward rush and were firing at the gunboats. Musketry crackled. Balls skipped and splashed into the sea. Fox ignored all that. He bent to the gun again and a blinding, stingingly nostalgic memory of that very first time he'd bent to Uncle Ebeneezer's punt-gun gushed up in him. There was no sweet Mary to hand the match to now, like a marshboy turned gentleman, and so give her the thrill of firing at the fluttering mass of ducks. Now they were French soldiers, aiming to shoot him down, and the load was grape, right up the muzzle and if the gun didn't burst he'd have the bastards ...

He touched the match to the touch-hole.

The gun concussed, banging splendidly and through the swirling acrid smoke Fox saw the next group of French infantry go down. The men set up a cheer. The British had cheered all along the line just before the boats grounded. Well, there was no time for another load. Here came the froggy bastards...

"Cutlasses, pikes, tomahawks!" roared Fox and the world went up in the air and turned over in the most elemental roaring as blackness shot through with flame engulfed him and he knew the boat had been hit and shattered into fragments and all his men scattered and — for him?

A moment of darkness and vivid scarlet agony, roaring and shrieking, and then water smashing into his face and gouging into his eyes and ears and nose and mouth, and the soft, gritty feel of sand beneath his outspread hands ...

Chapter Eleven

Someone was screaming close by.

Fumes and blood and darkness cleared from his right eye although his left had completely shut down. He saw Mr. Midshipman Hardcastle sitting shoulder deep in the water, holding his face from which the bright blood poured. Other seamen were struggling up, bloody and wounded. The shattered timbers of the boat scattered on the waters. A few trails of bubbles rose from the sinking two-pounder.

"Up, you blagskites!" Fox meant to roar. All that came out was a mere croak.

He stood up, shaking, swaying, feeling the sand sliding beneath his shoes.

"Ashore! Get ashore! Get stuck into the bastards!"

He had his cutlass in his fist. He waved it. The water dragged at his legs.

Ahead all was a confusion of reeling, struggling men, slashing and thrusting, with horses rearing and men screaming and falling. Scarlet and blue and green all mixed up together.

If this left flank gave way, if the dragoons broke the infantry here the whole beach was open to them. Backed by the fresh columns of infantry running down on to the beach from the dunes the French would sweep along as a broom sweeps, catching the toiling British in flank, roll them up until they penned the bloody remnants into the angle where the steep sandhills were covered by fire from the massed guns of the castle of Abukir.

The beach presented an incredible vision.

Spurting masses of smoke, the gleam of hundreds of weapons, the lines of scarlet struggling on, the masses of blue reluctantly falling back, the blobs of scarlet and blue upon the sands where the slain had fallen. It was all a chaotic senseless vision of hell.

This, hell or not, was a situation George Abercrombie Fox could understand, a situation for which he might have been born.

"On!" he yelled, rushing through the shallows. "Hit the bastards! Come on, Alkons!"

There were many more than Alkons fighting here, and a clump of men joined him in his savage onward rush.

They were waist high, they were knee high, they were ankle high, and then they were running clear of the water and falling upon the packed mass of writhing men.

The cutlass went in and out and a blue body contorted away. That cutlass no longer shone a brave silver; a greasy red stain along the blade grew thicker at each blow.

Fox slipped in blood, and recovered, and ducked and so let a sabre blow go swishing past above his head.

He leaped, got his left hand around the dragoon's belt. The sabre came down again and this time the cutlass blocked the descending blade. The horse screamed and reared. Fox hung on, wrenched the dragoon from his saddle, as he went down the cutlass plunged into his neck. The gay dragoon helmet jerked off and rolled away, the horsehair plumes draggling in wet sand. Fox sprang away and instantly found a bayoneted musket at his breast. He jerked sideways, let the spike go past, brought his knee up and then the cutlass down and chopped away the fellow's face.

A scarlet figure appeared at his side and Fox half-turned and kicked a musket away, saw a French soldier start to drive his bayonet into the unprotected back of the guardsman. Fox yelled:

"Ware your back!" and lunged forward. The kicked musket flew up and he was able to slide past and strike the Frenchman a clumsy blow. The guardsman swung about, all pressed up with a dragoon ineffectually trying to cut down on him. At Fox's second blow the infantryman collapsed.

"Thanks, mate!" yelled the guardsman. He drove in at the dragoon, put his bayonet into the man's thigh and into the horse's flank. The horse reared and the guardsman withdrew. Fox slashed at another who tried to chop down. For a space it was all cut and thrust and skip and dodge, and then, in one of those fractional, eerie, spaces in battle the guardsman and Fox were isolated among dead and wounded men.

Fox glared at the guardsman and ghostly memories stirred.

He was a sergeant, his three broad stripes ripped and bloodied. His scarlet uniform was a wreck. He was bareheaded. But the musket was firmly gripped in broad brown hands, and his plug-ugly face, with its broken nose and seamed cheeks showed the same fighting fury as animated everyone on this beach of blood.

Fox knew who had broken that nose.

Young Abe, and a broken bottle, down there in Rotherhithe by the Thames, and a silk kerchief the prize ...

"Hey, Jack," said Fox, swirling his cutlass so the red drops flew. "Heard from the Hogans lately?"

124

"Eh?" said the guards sergeant. "Who? What ... ?" He peered closer, looking into Fox's face. He drew back.

"Abe Fox!" He shook his head, not believing. "That black bastard Abe Fox, the very divil 'Imself!"

"Jack Coggan — so they made a soldier outta you!"

A dragoon charged them then and they both swung up to return to 1801, to a beach in Egypt, and to the strenuous business of fighting a battle. But — Jack Coggan! A crony of the hated Hogans, the family foes of the Foxes! How they had fought, gang against gang! They'd been kids, then; but the Hogans and Fox had not only patched up any old childish quarrel, they'd gone together on the high pad. Fox had heard that Jack Coggan had gone for a soldier, had taken the king's shilling, and they'd all laughed over that.

Now, here he was, a sergeant in the Second Guards, the regiment they called the Coldstream, bold as brass and fighting for his country against Jack Corse ... Well, well ...

In those old days the most hated enemy had been the family of Hogans and their allies. If, only last year, Fox had been brought up to date on the Hogan family history; the distressing news about young Kate and the disappearance of that Katie Hogan, young Katie's mother, who had been the first with whom Fox had rolled in his ivories, the quarrel with Lord Rowe and the interim vengeance exacted, the relaxed drinking they'd indulged in together, if so, well perhaps this fiery Sergeant Jack Coggan was not au fait with the current situation.

The French now made a most determined attack to tumble the British left flank into ruin. But with scarlet coats and blue coats jumbled together, and the green of the dragoons thinning, some kind of order was being restored. Fox noted with a deep exultation that the order was of the kind that would please Sir Ralph, and dreadfully disappoint the French general — Friant, scuttle-butt had his name.

The left flank was being held. The Coldstream, the 3rd Guards, the 54th, were forming up, long scarlet lines in dressing that held slanted musket barrels in perfect alignment.

Fox glared about, whipping the sweat from his forehead, his left eye blinking back to some kind of vision.

Hardcastle was there, bloody faced, a bloody sword in his fist. Others of the Alkons clustered. Now was the time to seek out Sir Sidney and start getting the guns into position. The few army artillery pieces that had been trundled ashore from the launches were in action; but more guns were needed.

The French were tumbling back among the wind-blown sandhills and very quickly they would reform and present another obstinate resistance.

Knowing the French, Fox guessed they'd come belting down out of the sand dunes in a moment, still confident of victory, still filled with that invincible fighting fury which animated them, come roaring down to undo all the advantage of the landing.

A hand grabbed Fox's left shoulder, under the epaulette, swung him around.

In sheer animal instinct the cutlass in Fox's right hand swept down and only in the last instant could he change the direction of the blow and so sweep it off sideways, away from the scarlet-faced soldier who gripped him in passionate fury.

"You, sir! You damned insolent bastard! I'll have you —"

"The honourable captain!" said Fox, aware of the battle bellowing on all about them, the rushing scarlet, the spurning clouds of smoke. This captain was not a guardsman. He looked dreadful.

"You scum! I'll have you broke and dismissed — I'll have you flogged out of the service — I'll ..."

"There's no time for a personal quarrel now, captain. Your place is with the troops, even if they aren't your regiment. We must take those dunes at once!"

"I'll not stand to take orders from an insolent guttersnipe like you ..."

Farther around to the left an eight-pounder's smoke showed over the dunes. The damned thing kept plumping right into the British. That had to be taken and silenced. Again the captain reached out a hand to grip Fox. Fox looked into that scarlet, sweating, pop-eyed face. He knew he wore his old devilish look, and he saw the soldier's reactions, the crinkle between the eyes, the flinching back, the wavering ...

"Take your hand off me, captain, or I'll knock your teeth down your throat."

"Sergeant!" The captain's words came out as a hoarse shriek, like a duck of the marshes trapped, and Sergeant Jack Coggan stepped up.

"Sir!" he bellowed in that guardsman's blank shout.

Coggan still gripped a musket. He must have picked it up when his own white-painted pike snapped. Now he stared with a hungry leer upon Fox as the captain said:

"This naval ... person ... is ..."

"There's no time for nonsense." Fox pointed at the smear of smoke above the dunes. "That must be ..."

The captain yelled again, words that spat out, mixed with froth upon his lips. He shook. He was completely out of control.

"We must take that gun," said Fox. He glared at Coggan. "Jack — come on!"

"Not so fast, Abe! At least he's an officer and a gentleman, which is moren' you are. You can't go round givin' orders —"

"To hell with you both!"

Fox started to run across the sand. He waved his cutlass and he bellowed.

"Alkons! Alkons!"

They were with him, Midshipman Hardcastle with the blood wet upon his face, Mr. Shaw, Horny Pete, a bunch of them, raving on over the sand. A scatter of soldiers followed. Fox ran hard, feeling the sand treacherous under his shoes, feeling the sweat thick and greasy upon him, the hot air dragged down into his lungs burning, burning ...

The French up there were shooting down.

The slope steepened. He attacked it with the ferocious zeal of a maniac, scrambling up, on hands and knees, forcing himself to go on and up. Musket balls spattered into the sand by his ears. He heard men shrieking as they were hit and fell, their screams close and high above the drum roll of battle all along this bloody beach.

The eight-pounder fired again.

This time the French gunners were using canister. The charge tore a dreadful gap in the upward thrusting ranks of scarlet. Fox drove himself on. His mad rush had taken him in a wild crabbing motion diagonally up the slope. It was almost impossible to progress straight up. He gave up waving his cutlass to encourage his men and set himself to negotiate the last few yards of the slope. The breath rattled in his throat. His eyes were starting from his head. Everything was whirling and roaring away in his skull.

Frantic impressions of blue and steel, of scarlet and orange flashes from the guns, of smoke belching, of men down with their guts torn out, men shrieking, horses rearing and screaming, a glimpse of fierce black moustaches in a brown Gallic face ...

Despite all the ferocious animal strength packed into his squat frame, Fox had to pause for a moment on the crest, dragging in huge whooping gasps of breath. His chest felt as though a thirty-two pounder's trucks had recoiled back over it.

Over there the gunners at the eight-pounder were jumping into frenzied action at the apparition of British sailors and soldiers on their own flank, when they had been gleefully shooting down into the flank of the British below.

The Frog gunners were a proficient lot. Fox knew that. They had the experience of whiffing away Turkish soldiers in hordes to buoy them up. The number one was frantically swinging his levers around from the transom of the tail. The numbers four and five were helping with their levers across the trail in their u-brackets. The number two was hopping about in front with the rammer — the Frogs called it the ecouvillon, a sponge and rammer combined. The number seven carried the single-piece charge — cartridge in its wooden sabot and tin canister of death tied to it — and was hurrying across to hand it to the number three.

Those gunners across there in their red-faced blue uniforms knew exactly what they were doing. Their infantry helpers were casting aside the artillery impediment in which they assisted and were scurrying for their muskets.

Fox took in all that busy scene of death in the fraction of a moment, in the time it took to inflate his massive chest twice. There was not a moment to be lost.

The soldiers-on his right were going forward now.

The men sent up a long howling cheer as they went up the slope. At least this eight-pounder wouldn't molest them further.

But it would do more than molest Fox and his motley band of jack tars and lobsters. It would whiff them into bloody gobbets.

Fox waved his cutlass, bellowed: "Follow me!" and ran just as fast as he could. He saw the gun appear to sway up and down as though he observed it from the deck of a water hoy off

Brest. That was a result of fatigue. God knew when he'd last slept,

Hardcastle, Horny Pete, Williamson, a gaggle of his men were with him. Shaw could keep up. The soldiers were there, their bayonets extended, slick with blood. Sergeant Jack Coggan was howling imbecilic, obscene words that meant nothing. They were going to make it — they were going to — Fox saw what was happening at that deadly eight-pounder: The French worked their guns on the Gribeauval system, and mighty effective they were, too. He calculated distances and what was going on as the charge was rammed, the number five pierced it and slid in the primer tube. Number four was swinging his linstock. Fox opened his mouth —

The linstock went down ...

"Down!" bellowed Fox. "Bury your faces in the sand!"

Down went his men of *Alkon* and the other seamen they'd picked up. Jack Coggan faltered, stared wildly at Fox. At Coggan's side the honourable captain, madly excited, his face ripe to bursting with passion, his blue eyes like cascabels, screeched.

"Cowardly dog! Charge! On! On!"

"Get your bloody fool head down, Jack!"

"Charge! Charge!" shrieked the honourable captain, rushing on, screaming, waving his sword. The soldiers followed him unhesitatingly.

The gun fired.

Fox saw it.

He saw the honourable captain's face vanish to be replaced by a butcher's slab of blood. He saw half a dozen guardsmen stagger and fall, yelling, he saw the blood, the dangling eyes, the smashed arms and legs, the scarlet uniforms all spattered with dark blood.

The captain was staggering about, his hands to that ghastly red smear between his ears.

Sergeant Jack Coggan remained upright, alive, unharmed; Fox leaped up.

"Alkons! Navy! Go get the bastards!"

With demoniac howls the seamen poured along the crest and their yells for a moment drowned the incessant uproar of musketry and cannon fire.

Fox ran past Jack Coggan.

"Come on, Jack!"

Fox took the honourable captain's shoulder as he ran past and pushed the poor devil down.

"Sit there, you stupid fool, and die out of the way of fighting men."

Over the sand, cutlasses and pikes and tomahawks brandished, muskets and bayonets slim and lethal — the French saw the game was up. They turned and ran, the red turnbacks of their coats twinkling among the blue.

"Give 'em a parting shot, Sarn't!" bellowed Fox.

Coggan's mouth was open, panting. But the tone of voice Fox used was perfectly familiar to him. Years of drill and discipline snapped into his shocked mind. He pattered out his orders and the guardsmen loaded and levelled and delivered their fire.

A few of the French fell.

The rest were swiftly vanishing.

Here came Mr. Shaw, panting and puffing; but Fox and the Alkons had the eight-pounder turned about using those cleverly convenient Frog levers. The charge looked odd with the tin canister fastened to the serge bag of powder. Fox knew that a handful of grass or straw or something should be thrust down first to act as a packing wad. The French, here on this sandy beach, had not trusted to finding grass enough and had broken bundles of dried stuff with them. Fox yelled and his men handled the piece in Navy fashion, and the match wrapped around the linstock touched the priming and the cannon banged away.

Mr. Shaw began bellowing to reload.

Fox said: "You may reload with great pleasure, Mr. Shaw. There are no targets left for us here. And the army are all ashore over there."

Mr. Shaw looked most disgruntled.

"Missed all the bleeding fun," he said.

Ripe insubordination that might be. Fox found this close contact with the army unsettling; they were a confounded indisciplinary bunch, the men forming a kind of anarchic and yet strictly controlled realm of their own, quite unknown to their officers. Yet he let Mr. Shaw grumble on. He walked a little way off. Yes, it had been done.

The British Army had got ashore, had successfully charged the French and run them out of their positions. It had been a victory.

Bigod! A victory, a real genuine triumph!

The boats of the fleet were pulling line by line for the shore bearing the second division. The whole animated scene took on an abruptly different complexion. Consolidation of the position so gallantly won must be the next concern, and then it would be forward, on to Alexandria!

Fox felt the edges of weariness enwrap him. Tiredness was a mortal sin in a sea officer, an insult to the men under his command.

The soldiers were reforming, exultant, the mood of elation and victory charging the air. Above them the sky beamed down, blue and serene, the sea moved in its glassy stillness, the sand grains tumbled underfoot.

"Not a bleeder to shoot this little lot at," Mr. Shaw was grumbling away.

Fox turned.

"Mr. Hardcastle! You'll vastly oblige me by going and having that confounded face of yours seen to — d'you want a scar to frighten the girls, hey?"

"N — no, sir. Aye aye, sir!"

Mr. Midshipman Hardcastle gulped and hared away, sliding and scrabbling down the sand dunes.

The French foot artillery men had got off, with their caissons, the horses galloping with bloody flanks; and the limbers, mere two wheel platforms for the trail pintles, were no great prize. Still: "You'd better secure the gun, Mr. Shaw."

"Aye aye, sir." The gunner went about his work, fussing and yet perfectly competent, as Fox observed.

Sergeant Jack Coggan observed, in his turn, that ferocious seamed visage of Abe Fox, that phizog that could curdle the milk in a wet-nurse's breast. Sergeant Coggan began to sweat a trifle.

What had he been saying to the Royal Naval officer? Abe had an epaulette. These jack tars jumped when he spoke.

Now Fox turned that intemperate ice-floe glance of his on the Coldstream sergeant.

"Sarn't! I'll trouble you to step over here."

"Yessir!"

Together, a little apart from the others, standing on the crest with the sweep of Abukir Bay below, the fort away to their left, the sea before them, and the impressive tangle of masts of the fleet and the busy activity of boats between fleet and shore, Fox spoke in a reflective tone.

"You are a sergeant of the Coldstream, and I am a commander in the Royal Navy. If you want to continue any little misunderstandings we experienced as children you may do so. We will find a place and time convenient to us both. I shall take off my coat and you yours. It'll be man against man. Well, sarn't? What have you to say?"

The sun was climbing the blue. The beach swarmed with men. There was work to be done.

"I saw, Abe, that orficer — a gennelman, he was — and —"

"And he's dead, the bloody idiot ... Speak up!"

"It was a long time ago, Abe. Let bygones be bygones, eh?"

"Correct. I'll find your bivouac some time and we'll split a bottle. You'll want to hear about Katie Hogan, and all the rest. Now, sarn't —" And here, despite all the ghostly memories of the reeking streets and the eternal smells of tar and bilge-water and cabbage, of the sweep of the marshes, of his brother Johnny, of the gangs and the tangy nostalgic heart-rending oldness of his youth, Fox's voice cracked out in your true Royal Naval foretop hailing voice.

"Cut along, sarn't!"

"Yessir!"

And Sergeant Jack Coggan doubled off, back to join his regiment.

Fox watched him go. A part of his own life went there.

The victory had been won, here, this day. Bonaparte's veterans had met British redcoats and had run. Was that an omen for the future? Had the despised British Army found its soul, here on the bloody beach of Abukir Bay?

George Abercrombie Fox swung back to the demands of the present. He knew what needed to be done. Sir Sidney would bring down the wrath of the Lord God Almighty if Fox failed him now, after prating with such high promises.

Strange, how meeting an old foe of his youth, a childhood enemy, had thrown everything into perspective. There must be thousands of Jack Coggans in this army. Fox fancied there were not thousands of Foxes in the navy. Bigod! He hoped not — what the service would come to if there were boggled his mind.

He had not been fortunate enough to sail with Nelson into the Baltic; he rather fancied that what had been accomplished here would take a lot of beating. But then, he knew Nelson, he knew the little admiral would roll in every rig, he knew he'd do something glorious and fine and a deed to fill the country with clamour.

Well, Fox had done what he had set out to do. He'd brought his flute safely to anchor. He'd done his duty in the boats, saved lives, got the men ashore. He'd covered the flank and taken a gun, he'd seen Monsieur Jean Crapaud off in lively fashion. There was more yet to be done; as he walked back to his men, Fox wondered if ever a time would come when there was never anything still to be done.

With a grim deliberate tread and that look of the devil upon his face, George Abercrombie Fox walked back to take command of his men and drive them forward into whatever of terror and adventure and loot Egypt might hold for them.

THE END

If you enjoyed this book, look for others like it at Thunderchild Publishing: http://www.ourworlds.net/thunderchild/

Made in the USA
Middletown, DE
05 April 2021